Phil Redmond's

HOLLYOAKS
A MERSEY TELEVISION COMPANY

SEEING RED

SELF-HARM

Self-harming is basically any sort of action which involves injuring your own body. Cutting is one form of self-harm, but some people may burn or hit themselves, pull out their hair or pick at their skin. Heavy drinking, drug-taking or severe eating disorders are also forms of self-harm. For some people, self-harm is sometimes the only way they can find to deal with great emotional distress. People who self-harm often feel ashamed and isolated, and try to keep what they are doing a secret. Self harming is not attention seeking, and it's important not to be critical or hostile towards someone you are supporting if they are self-harming.

If you are worried about self-harming, it's important that you get help. Try to speak to someone you can trust. If you would rather speak to some-one you don't know, you can phone a helpline and get help and advice from people who understand what is happening to you.

Children and young people up to 18 can speak to someone at **Childline** about anything which is causing them distress. You can phone them on 0800 11 11 at any time of the day or night. Calls are free and confidential. The lines can be really busy, so you may need to ring a few times before you get through. There's lots of useful information on Childline's website including help for bullying and sexual abuse at www.childline.org.uk

If you are having trouble coping, **The Bristol Crisis Service for Women** offers a helpline, booklets and information on local services for any woman in distress, particularly about self-harm. For information write to BCSW, P O Box 654, Bristol, BS99 1XH. You can phone them on Fridays and Saturdays between 9pm and 12.30am and on Sundays from 6pm to 9pm on 0117 925 1119. Check out their website at: www.users.zetnet.co.uk/bcsw

Young Minds is a charity which provides information and support to young people and their parents on a range of mental health issues. **Young Minds** produces a number of booklets especially for young people, including one about self-injury, and others about depression, sexual abuse, bullying and eating disorders. You can find these leaflets and other helpful information on their website at www.youngminds.org.uk Or write to them for free copies with a stamped self addressed envelope to: Young Minds, 102-108 Clerkenwell Road, London EC1M 5SA

Youth Access offers details of local advice, information and counselling services on a variety of issues including sexual abuse, bullying, self-harm and other subjects. Phone them on 020 8772 9900 on weekdays between 9am and 5pm.

If your family is going through a difficult time and you are in a parent-ing role, you can get free and confidential help on any issue from **Parentline Plus**. Their helpline is open 24 hours a day on 0808 800 22 22, or visit the website at www.parentlineplus.org.uk

You can phone the Samaritans at any time of the day or night to talk in confidence about your feelings. You can contact the **Samaritans** on 08457 90 90 90 or via their website at www.samaritans.org

You can check out the Channel 4 website at channel4.com/health for information on all sorts of topics and the opportunity to ask confidential questions.

Phil Redmond's

HOLLYOAKS

A MERSEY TELEVISION COMPANY

SEEING RED

KADDY BENYON

First published 2002 by Channel 4 Books
an imprint of Pan Macmillan Ltd
Pan Macmillan, 20 New Wharf Road, London N1 9RR
Basingstoke and Oxford
Associated companies throughout the world
www.panmacmillan.com

ISBN 0 7522 6475 3

1 3 5 7 9 8 6 4 2

A CIP catalogue record for this book is
available from the British Library.

Photographs © Hollyoaks Productions Limited 2002

Typeset by seagulls
Printed and bound in Great Britain by Mackays of Chatham

Lisa Hunter bursts out of the school hall and into the dark and deserted playground. The weighted door slowly closes on the music and laughter that spills out behind her until the only sound she hears is her heart beating, fast and unsteady.

The shock has made her woozy and she thinks she might faint. Groaning, she closes her eyes and leans on a teacher's car to steady herself. The urge to throw up comes over her suddenly and there is nothing she can do to stop it. It starts as a burp, but in seconds she is gagging and her mouth and nose fill with a rush of hot, bitter liquid. It gushes down the side of the car, collecting in a mustard-coloured pool at her feet. She gasps for air, as if she's been swimming under water for too long. It makes her cough and strings of spit hang from her swollen, red lips.

She doesn't dare move, but after a few moments she weakly lifts her head away from the acrid smell which is working its way up her nostrils and making her feel nauseous again. Her prom queen tiara has slipped from her newly highlighted hair and snags awkwardly above her right ear. She pulls it free and hurls it to the ground, crushing it with the toe of her sister's fake Manolos.

She wipes her mouth with her stole as she pads unsteadily over to the water fountain. She scrapes her hair behind her neck and sucks in a huge mouthful of disappointingly warm water. She swills it around her mouth and spits it out, desperate to rid herself of the taste of sick.

Suddenly, the music from the hall grows loud again and behind her she hears her classmates having a great time. Lisa braces herself, knowing she is no longer alone. She screws her eyes shut and hopes whoever it is will go away, but the sound of footsteps drawing closer makes her panic. She starts to run, not knowing where she is going, not caring; she just has to get away.

After a while, somewhere a million miles behind her, she hears someone following her. Her boyfriend Brian pants her name, begging her to come back. He sounds more distant than he probably is and pathetic like a whining dog. If she turned and looked at him, maybe he'd stop. If he could just touch her, hold her once more, maybe she wouldn't feel like she was dying. But he did this; he humiliated her in front of the whole school and ruined everything.

Anger sears through her veins. She doesn't want to turn and see his beautiful face. If she does, she knows she will crumble. Determined not to let him see what he has done to her, she runs so hard her chest burns and her feet start to blister. But she doesn't care about the pain. She just has to get home to where it's safe.

* * *

She's not sure what time it is, but her feet are killing her and she's freezing cold. Breathless, she lets herself into the house and stands still in the darkness, listening to see if anyone's around. Satisfied she's got the place to herself, she hitches her dress up and runs up the stairs two at a time, darting into her bedroom and locking the door.

Still trying to regain her breath and choking on tears, she pulls the second drawer of her dressing table off its runners and empties it onto the floor. Taped to the underside of the drawer is an old tin pencil-case. Lisa rips it free and opens it with shaking hands, careful not to spill its contents.

A small pair of silver nail scissors twinkles up at her, nestling on a bed of gauze and sachets of Savlon wipes. Lisa bites her lip as she gently takes them out and carries them over to the bed. She sits cross-legged on her duvet, all the while cupping the precious objects in her hands, never taking her eyes off them. She leans forward and lays them on her pillow, like a row of fragile dolls.

Feeling guilty about what she is going to do, she half-heartedly tries to talk herself out of it. But then she remembers what Brian did. She trusted him and he threw it back in her face. To think, tonight she was going to sleep with him. Her nose tingles again, signalling the arrival of more hot, salty tears. They course down her cheeks, dragging glitter and mascara with them. She tries to suffocate a yelp of pain banging on the wall of her chest, but she can feel it rising up inside her, like a huge throbbing knot of despair.

With a shaking hand, she reaches for the scissors, sharp and cool. She opens them and rests her little finger between the blades. She tentatively squeezes them, just enough so the surrounding skin turns white. In that moment, she feels like she has harnessed the pain bucking around inside her like a wild horse.

Shakily she exhales, but chokes again as the sight of Brian and Zara snogging flashes into her mind. She squeezes her eyes tight shut and shakes her head from side to side, trying to dislodge the image, but it won't go. It sticks fast, silently taunting her.

She releases her finger from its trap and looks at the scissors. She closes her eyes and holds the scissors against her cheek, soothing the hot tracks of her tears. She gently moves them, lifting her chin to let them caress her neck, and then, with two hands, holds them tight against her chest, like the biggest secret in the world. Her heart beats faster and the knot inside begins to grow and ache again, as if it knows it will soon be undone.

Lisa pulls the handles of the scissors slowly apart, enjoying the sound of metal grinding against metal. She clasps the left blade down upon the left handle and lowers the point of the other blade towards her arm. Her fist clenches in anticipation and she gasps when the metal scratches her skin. She drags it softly, chalking a pattern of mock scars. She puts the scissors down and examines her handiwork, then realizes she doesn't feel any better.

Disgusted with herself, she tries to fight the temptation. She gets up from the bed and walks across the room. Music. Music would be good. She plays the CD she had ready for her and Brian. But it doesn't soothe away the pain; it makes it ten times worse. She holds her arms tightly around herself, as if trying to hug it all better.

Wherever she looks, wherever she stands in the room, she can see the scissors out of the corner of her eye, calling her. She looks away, anywhere, everywhere. Suddenly her pin board is the most fascinating thing in the room. She knows she has to concentrate on something else. She sees her old revision timetable, ruthlessly optimistic. She pulls it down, screws it into a ball and chucks it on the floor. When she looks back at the board, she stops dead. There he is, looking adoringly back at her: Brian.

Lisa grits her teeth as she glares at him. How could he do this to her? Her heart beats faster and she bites the inside of her mouth, determined not to cry again. But it's too big for her; the pain is gathering and rising like a storm inside and she only knows one way to deal with it.

She turns to the bed and lunges for the scissors. This time there's no time for pretty patterns. She pushes the point of the blade in until she feels it bite, then drags it slowly along her arm, deeper than ever before. Small beads of red appear and Lisa is pleased to see them, but they're not enough. She cuts again and again.

The blood rushes up to greet her and crimson tears spill down either side of her arm. She stares at them blankly, watching them glisten in the light and trickle into an intricate labyrinth. She dips into the droplets with the tip of her index finger, playing with them, enjoying them. She knows it should hurt, but it doesn't. All she feels is numb, numb and relieved.

Lisa swaddles her cuts in gauze and reluctantly mops the blood away, knowing as a dull sting starts to throb under the skin that it's time to pack her secret away again. She cradles her shredded and shiny limb, and waits for the ripped seams of her life to congeal and hold themselves back together until next time. But the blood keeps pumping up to the surface, oozing out of her.

***

She starts to feel worried when after ten minutes the blood is still coming, thick and fast. The gauze has become saturated and the Savlon wipes are all gone. She holds her other hand over the gashes, vaguely remembering from first aid that applying pressure might stem the flow. It seems to work for a moment, then the rivulets of red seep through the spaces between her fingers and gather there, threatening to spill onto her new dress.

Lisa panics and jumps up, heading for her wardrobe, where she keeps a supply of cotton wool. She feels dizzy and the room starts to spin. She knows she is swaying and tries to focus on something, anything. But it is too late. Everything goes black and Lisa crashes to the floor.

ONE

It sends shivers through me now, when I think about how bad my life seemed then. It started before we moved to the new house, but got much worse when I had to change school. My first day at Hollyoaks Comp was a nightmare. All the other kids had known each other since year seven at least, some since primary school. Why would any of them have wanted to make friends with a freak like me?

Mum had made my dad promise he'd drop me off in the van. That was the kiss of death, really. I mean, I was fourteen and getting escorted to school – talk about embarrassing. Everyone was going to think I was a right baby. He tooted when he drove off as well. I might as well have had a neon sign on my head with an arrow saying, 'new girl'.

So there I was, feeling stupid and alone in my stiff new uniform. Mum had sewn the school badge onto my blazer in a hurry, as she waited for her taxi to take her to the airport. It was wonky and I tried to cover it up with the strap of my bag, but it kept slipping, so I gave up.

I didn't know where the hell I was meant to be, so I banked on finding the office. Some spotty boy grunted and pointed me in the direction when I asked him. He didn't even look me in the eye long enough for me to say thanks. I became worried that he might be a typical specimen of the boys at this school and my heart sank.

After rifling through reams of messy paperwork, the lady in the office managed to find out my form teacher was Mr Bennet. Nice name, I thought, as she told me to sit down and wait for him to come and get me. I wondered if he would be young and good-looking. As other teachers came and went, they all stared at me, wondering what I had done. I felt like explaining this wasn't a punishment, but then, it did feel like one.

Mr Bennet turned out to be pale and stringy with loads of moles. He skidded into the office as if he hadn't had time to stop hurrying. He was about forty and his hair needed a really good cut. I had to jog along beside him in the corridors to keep up.

Everyone stopped talking and stared at me when I walked into the classroom. Mr Bennet introduced me to the class. Some of them said hello when he prompted them, but most had lost interest by then and returned to their conversations.

'Quiet please while I take the register,' Mr Bennet said, as he sat on the corner of his desk and started marking names off. I felt stupid, standing there like a lemon. Had he forgotten about me already? I gently cleared my throat to get some attention, knowing from the heat in my cheeks I'd already got it from a group of girls sniggering at my discomfort at the back of the room.

Mr Bennet looked up, mildly irritated and told me to sit next to a really pretty blonde girl. I smiled at her nervously, but she just looked at me, leaning back on her chair and blowing a perfect pink bubble. I watched it grow bigger and bigger, then jumped a little when it burst, covering her cherry-red lips.

'Want some?' she said, smiling sweetly. She let her chair fall forward again as she peeled it back into her mouth with her teeth.

I shook my head.

'I'm Steph, by the way. What's your name again? Lucy?' she asked.

'Lisa,' I corrected.

'Shame,' she said. 'My brother's girlfriend's called Lisa and she's a right bitch.'

I didn't know what to say to that. Was I meant to apologize for having a name she didn't like or something? I listened to the other names being called out and tried to match them to faces. It wasn't long before I was totally confused.

I sensed Steph jolt beside me, and turned to see her giving the finger to the girl behind who had just poked her in the back with a ruler.

'Aren't you going to introduce us?' said the girl, nodding her eyes at me. She wasn't as pretty as Steph and looked quite tough. She too had loads of make-up on and a dog collar around her neck. I smiled at her and she blanked me. So did the frizzy-haired girl in the leather jacket sitting next to her.

'Zara and Abby,' Steph said, sounding totally bored as she pointed by throwing a thumb over her shoulder at each of them in turn.

'Hi,' I said, looking hopefully from one to the other for a glimmer of compassion. But I found none, just two pairs of dark eyes boring into me.

The bell rang and Steph shoved her magazine into her bag, scraped her chair back and sauntered off to her first lesson, Zara and Abby not far behind.

'What do you think?' I heard Zara say.

'Not much,' said Steph, with a loud snap of her gum.

'She's a bit of a mouse, isn't she?' said Abby as they rounded the corner and disappeared.

I felt disappointed. They'd hardly given me much of a chance before they wrote me off. I sighed as I looked at the photocopied timetable Mr Bennet had given me. French next – great, my worst subject.

As I was about to leave, a boy I hadn't noticed before smiled at me as he locked a guitar into his locker at the back of the room.

'Don't worry about them. They're not half as fierce as they make out,' he said.

'I'm not worried,' I said defensively. 'I just think they're rude.'

He chuckled at this and I realized I must have sounded snotty, but at least it broke the ice.

'I'm Brian,' he said, extending a hand.

'Lisa,' I smiled, shaking it, and thinking what lovely brown eyes he had.

* * *

I made it through morning lessons without having a clue what was going on. No one spoke to me, but I could sense Steph, Abby and Zara watching me with lazy interest. I kept my head down in French, praying I wouldn't get asked a question. Mrs Starkey terrified me and I was counting the minutes to lunchtime. Finally, the bell rang and we were set free, though not before being given a huge translation as homework.

While wondering how to get to the canteen, I spotted Zara coming out of the toilets by the art room. I tried not to lose her in the bustle as I hurried to catch up. I was too scared to talk to her; she hadn't seemed over-friendly before, so I walked along behind her, trying to make it look like I wasn't following. Suddenly she turned around and I almost went crashing into her.

'Are you following me?'

She looked annoyed. Oh God, not an enemy already? As I considered the best way to appease her, her face cracked into a smile and she nudged me with her elbow. 'Kidding,' she said. 'Blimey, somebody needs to lighten up!'

I smiled with relief and she linked her arm in mine. 'Come on, everyone's outside. I'll introduce you.' She led me into the playground, where some boys from our class were having a kick about. As I scanned their faces, looking for Brian, one of them deliberately knocked the ball into my back. Zara kicked it violently into the street.

'What did you go and do that for?' he wailed.

'Bite me,' Zara spat back at him as we walked on. We headed past the netball pitch and behind the swimming pool. On the grass, some sitting, some lying, was a group of kids I recognized from our class.

'Everyone, this is Lisa. She's new. Be nice.' With that, she plonked herself down next to a sunbathing Steph and patted the grass in an invitation for me to join her.

'So how come your badge is all wonky?' asked Abby, rolling onto her tummy, looking me up and down, and chewing a blade of grass.

'My mum did it in a hurry before she left for the airport,' I mumbled, realizing, a little too late, that I might have opened a can of worms I'd have rather kept tightly shut.

'Where's she gone?' asked Zara.

'Ibiza,' I said, breaking eye contact and hoping she wouldn't ask any more.

'Kickin',' said Steph in a stupid voice from under her shades. Everybody laughed. I felt like she was taking the mick, but smiled anyway. I didn't want to get defensive about it.

'Is she into clubbing or something?' asked Zara giggling.

'No,' I said, willing her to drop the subject. 'It's her job. She travels all over the place.' I knew as soon as it was out there I couldn't take it back, but I couldn't tell them the truth, not yet.

'What as, a pole dancer?' sniggered Steph.

'Yeah right,' I said, laughing as casually as I could. There was an awkward silence as they waited for me to tell them more, but how could I elaborate on a lie like that?

I knew I wasn't doing myself any favours by not trying to get to know them, but I felt shy and to be honest, more than a bit intimidated. Zara tried to make polite conversation for a while, but even she got fed up after a few monosyllabic answers. Soon she, too, lay back. I felt odd sitting in silence with three girls I didn't know as they sunbathed. I could have kicked myself.

A few moments later, Zara propped herself up on her elbows and looked over my shoulder, bored. Suddenly she grinned.

'Here comes sex on legs,' she whispered, looking at a boy coming over from the canteen. I craned my neck to see, but the sun was in my eyes. Zara jumped up and flung her arms around him, kissing him full on the lips. 'This is my boyfriend,' she said, proudly presenting him to me. He moved closer and obscured the sun. Only then did I see, with great disappointment, that it was Brian.

'Hello again,' he said.

I smiled at him, shielding my eyes with my hand.

'Oh, you've already met?' asked Zara.

'Yeah,' I mumbled, upset that the one decent boy had been snapped up already. I felt stupid for what I'd said about Zara before. Why hadn't he told me he was her boyfriend?

'You got us the tickets for that gig yet, Bri?' asked Steph without looking at him or sitting up.

'I'm working on it,' he replied.

'You know that trip to London next week?' asked Zara. I nodded. I'd been given a form in History that morning. 'We're all going to sneak out once the teachers have gone to bed and go to his cousin's gig,' she said, nodding in Brian's direction.

'Is it going to be any good?' asked Abby.

'Should be, yeah,' he answered.

'What kind of music is it?' I asked meekly.

They all looked at me, as if communally wondering whether they should invite me. I wasn't after an invitation; just conversation would have done.

'Oh, you know, nu metal mostly,' said Brian uncertainly; I think he didn't think I knew what it was. 'Do you want to come?' he asked, looking at Zara for reassurance this was okay. She shrugged.

'I don't know,' I said, not wanting to get into any trouble, but not wanting them to think I was a wimp at the same time. Luckily the bell rang. With a bit of prompting from the teacher on duty, we all stood up, brushed the grass off our clothes and ambled back inside, reluctant to leave the summer afternoon behind. Brian ran to catch up with me.

'It's five quid a ticket – are you in?' he asked, his voice guarded from teachers' ears, his eyes dark and serious.

'Sure,' I said, not sure at all how I was going to convince Dad to let me go.

TWO

It was cool and misty for a summer morning when I arrived at school on the day of the trip. Mr Bennet made us stand by the gates as he took the register and we waited for the coach to arrive. I had a bad feeling in the pit of my stomach. Maybe I shouldn't have listened to Zara after all, but she'd convinced me it was such a good idea at the time.

She came up with the plan in registration, a few days after I told her that my dad wouldn't let me go. She couldn't believe anyone's dad couldn't be talked round and immediately took it upon herself to make him change his mind.

'I've got a great plan,' she whispered excitedly. 'How about you fake your dad's signature on the form?' She was obviously pleased with herself.

'I could do,' I said, less enthusiastically. 'But how am I going to pay? I haven't got forty quid.' Zara's face dropped to mirror mine. I was secretly pleased I'd found a way out.

'I'll lend it to you,' she said brightly, a moment later.

'Since when did you have forty quid?' demanded Abby without lifting her eyes from copying Hannah Walker's homework.

'Since my dad started feeling totally guilty about the divorce,' Zara told her with pleasure. Steph looked up from filing her nails, impressed.

'So how about it?' she said, nudging me, as if she'd just solved all my problems.

'I'm not sure,' I said, and I wasn't. Sometimes it's just not worth winding my dad up. I mean, he's fine most of the time, but sometimes he just loses it and you know not to provoke him. He was always worse when Mum was away. I think he got a bit stressed about having to look after me and my brothers on his own or something. He said it was 'cos he missed Mum, and when he missed her he drank, and when he drank he was unbearable.

'Come on, what's there to think about? It'll be great,' enthused Zara, an edge of impatience in her voice.

'Yeah, until my dad realizes I haven't come home and comes looking for me.'

'He's hardly going to follow you to London,' said Abby patronizingly.

'You don't know my dad.' I wished they'd all just drop it.

' Tell him it's for a vital piece of coursework. I'll talk to him for you,' offered Zara.

'No!' I blurted out, a little too soon. 'Anyway, what's the big deal if I come or not?' I said, feeling rattled. 'It's not as if you really want me there,' I added, looking at Zara accusingly. I suppose I was really talking about Steph and Abby.

'Woo, moody,' Steph sang, enjoying my discomfort.

'I was only trying to help,' said Zara sulkily. I knew I'd hurt her feelings.

I didn't have any lessons with her that afternoon until P.E. last thing. She ignored me in the changing rooms and chatted with Steph and Abby, acting like I wasn't there. I felt pretty gutted and wondered if I had blown it with them.

I sat miserably on the bench at the side of the gym while Mrs Mitchell got Megan Bowers to demonstrate a safe dismount from the trampoline. I wasn't really listening, instead trying to catch Zara's eye to offer her a reconciliatory smile. Suddenly, a whistle blew in my face and I felt like my eardrums were going to burst. Mrs Mitchell was standing in front of me in her green tracksuit bottoms, with her hands on her hips. She didn't look happy.

'Well, Lisa … is it or isn't it?' she demanded, her eyes cold and hard.

'Erm,' I said, trying to buy myself more time. I had no idea what she was talking about. She warned me to pay attention and shook her head as she went to retrieve her answer from some other poor sod. She went on for a bit longer, then split us up into groups to practise on the four trampolines. I was in the same group as Zara and co., and took the opportunity to make amends – well, with Zara at least.

'I'm sorry about before,' I said as I leaned on the red plastic padding. 'I didn't mean to have a go. It's just that my dad's a right stick-in-the-mud. He won't let me do anything.' She looked at me without smiling and I wondered what else I could say or do.

'Did I tell you I was new here last year?' she asked. I shook my head. I had no idea. 'It took me ages to make friends and settle in. I wouldn't want it to be like that for you.' She looked at me and I couldn't read her expression. Was this some kind of warning or did she really care?

'I know,' I said. 'Listen, as long as you really don't mind lending me the money, then I suppose it won't hurt to try.'

'Wicked,' she grinned, as she scrambled onto the side of the trampoline and pulled herself upright. She wobbled over to Steph and bum-nudged her as she started jumping. 'Oi you, my turn,' she said, just as Mrs Mitchell blew her whistle and headed over.

* * *

None of the others was there yet, I noted as I shivered by the school gates. It wasn't too late for me to change my mind. There were other kids not going. Mostly the freaks and geeks though, I thought with dismay, until it dawned on me I'd probably fit right in with that lot.

I saw Zara and Brian hand-in-hand in the distance and realized it was too late to change my mind. I watched them before they saw me, wondering how they ever got it together. Zara's kind of loud and bossy, and from what I could tell, Brian was much more reserved and gentle.

'All set?' Zara said as they drew closer. I nodded weakly. 'Got away from your evil dad okay then?' she joked.

'He didn't suspect a thing,' I replied uneasily. 'Dan's going to cover for me.'

'Who's Dan?' asked Brian.

'My brother,' I told them.

'Is he good-looking?' asked Abby eagerly, coming up behind me.

'I don't know,' I answered. How are you meant to answer a question like that?

'Well, does he get much action or is he a total mong?'

Steph butted in. I didn't know, did I? I mean, there are some things that you just don't talk about with brothers and their love lives is one of them.

The coach pulled up and Mr Bennet told us to form a queue and wait while he talked to the driver. Then after a few minutes we were allowed to get on. Steph elbowed her way in front of me, desperate to nab the back seat. As if the new girl's going to try and hog the back seat all to herself.

I felt much better once we were on our way and even started to feel excited. Maybe this was going to work; maybe I was going to have a really good time with my new friends.

Zara surfaced from a snogging and whispering session with Brian on the back seat and called me over to join them. I stood in the aisle, leaning on the arm of Jamie Griffith's seat. He hadn't noticed; he was too busy texting rude messages to some spod at the front. Brian reached into his pocket and gave me my ticket for the gig.

'So we're really going to do this?' I asked, staring at it and reading the names of the bands on the front.

'Uh huh.' He nodded and smiled. I liked the way his hair flopped over his eyes.

The coach started to slow down and pulled into a lay-by.

'Oh God, has Heidi puked already?' Steph shouted up to the front of the coach. Mr Bennet told her to be quiet as he stood up to speak to the driver about what was wrong. She pulled a face at the back of his head and everyone laughed. I made my way back to my seat.

I casually looked out of the window I was leaning on, and was horrified to see a white van just like my dad's flashing its lights and pulling up behind us. I sank lower into my seat, hoping against hope that this didn't mean what I thought it did.

'What's going on?' someone shouted as Steph initiated a round of 'Why Are We Waiting?'. I felt sick. There was nowhere to hide, nothing I could do. My stomach knotted as I waited for the inevitable scene. He strode up to the side of the coach, Dan jogging along behind him. He saw me looking at him and glared. I knew I was in serious trouble.

Although I couldn't hear anything, I could see he was having a massive go at Mr Bennet. Everyone else could, too. They were intrigued and were leaning three-deep, noses against the windows, trying to hear what was being said. There was nothing I could do, but sit in one of the empty seats and wait. A few moments later, a very disgruntled Mr Bennet made his way back on board.

'Where's Lisa Hunter?' he asked, crossly. I looked at my feet, hoping I'd see some kind of trapdoor and be able to escape. I looked behind me, biting my lip. Everyone was staring. I closed my eyes and swallowed hard as I gingerly lifted my hand and stood up. 'Your father would like a word,' he said curtly. I gave him a half-smile, but he really wasn't in the mood.

Everyone started whispering among themselves as I gathered my things together.

'What's going on, Lise?' probed Zara gently. I couldn't look at her; I couldn't look at any of them. I was so red and tears were burning my eyes, threatening to spill over at any moment. I made my way to the front of the coach, where my dad was waiting for me, grim-faced.

'Hi Dad,' I said, trying to make out everything was okay and there really was no reason why everyone should be so enthralled.

Dad grabbed the top of my arm way too tight. Did he really think I'd try to make a break for it?

'Please, don't make a scene,' I whimpered, looking at all the open-mouthed faces staring at me. But he wasn't listening and I was dragged down the steps and off the coach.

'Sorry about this, but she has to learn,' he said to Mr Bennet, who nodded, knowing he could do nothing. I heard the door hiss closed behind us as Dan came over.

'I'm sorry,' he said. 'I tried to talk him out of it.' He obviously appreciated the utter humiliation being inflicted on me. I couldn't speak to him. I ran over to the van, got in and burst into tears. Dad was still yelling at Dan about interfering. I zoned out for a bit. The worst, most embarrassing thing in the world had just happened to me and pretty soon the whole school would know.

I looked up to see the coach pulling away and saw Zara kneeling on the back seat looking at me with concern. Abby was next to her, grinning and waving at me as she whispered something in Steph's ear. Steph laughed and blew a kiss at Dan. How would I ever be able to face them again?

THREE

They had a great time without me. I didn't stop hearing about it for weeks. I hated the fact that I'd missed out. It made me feel like I'd lost the chance to bond with everyone. My classmates were pleasant enough to me afterwards, but it was always accompanied by a look of sympathy. It took me ages to live it down and Abby was especially brutal in her teasing. There was no way she was going to let it drop until she'd made me feel as bad as she possibly could.

In public, Zara laughed along with her. In private, she sympathized with me. One day in Chemistry, I asked her why she thought Abby was giving me such a hard time. She said Abby was probably jealous. I waited for her to elaborate as I ignited the Bunsen burner, but she didn't carry on. I made a mental note to get to know Abby better. Maybe then she'd ease up on me a bit? I didn't tell Zara about my plan. I didn't want to give her the chance to try and change my mind.

The next day, Dan dropped me at school early because he had to get to the wholesaler's and back before the garage opened. It was weird being there before anyone else, kind of spooky. The corridors sounded all echoey and

I noticed things I never had before, like the walls. I'd never really taken in what a gross shade of green they were.

I went into the cloakroom to hang up my blazer and go to the loo. I was anxious about using these loos when no one was around as Steph reckoned they were haunted. Apparently, some girl was killed when she pulled the chain and the whole cistern fell on her head. I shuddered at the thought of it.

I was relieved when I heard someone else come in, but concerned when I thought I heard them crying. I stayed still for a moment, listening out but whatever it was had stopped, so I flushed the loo (careful not to stand underneath the cistern) and unlocked the door.

As I was washing my hands, something in the mirror caught my eye. Something had moved; I was sure of it. I turned around and couldn't see anything, but the hairs on the back of my neck stood on end and my skin broke out in goose bumps. I hurried back into the cloakroom, to get my stuff and get the hell out of there.

As I grabbed my bag, it caught on one of the wire shoe racks under the benches. I knelt down to release it, leaning on what I thought was someone's gym bag to steady myself, but then the gym bag yelped and so did I. I pulled back someone's art shirt hanging on a hook to see Abby sitting behind it, the gym bag on her knee.

'What are you doing in there?' I asked, amused at her hiding.

'What's it to you?' she retorted defensively.

'Sorry,' I said. 'I was only asking.'

'Well, don't,' she snapped back.

Sick of Abby and her attitude, I was just about to give up on her, but then I noticed she'd been crying.

'Are you okay?' I ventured.

'Fan-tastic,' she replied sarkily. I took a breath, determined not to lose my rag with her.

'If you're upset, I might be able to help,' I offered, sitting down beside her.

'What would you know?' she said, shifting away from me. I sighed and got up to leave. She could be a right bitch sometimes. I headed for the door.

'Lisa?'

I turned, hopeful of a breakthrough. 'You'd better not tell anyone about this,' she spat.

'What's there to tell?' I was getting annoyed with her now. 'I don't even know what the hell's wrong with you.' I regretted it as soon as it was out of my mouth. I knew this would make her fly at me. But to my surprise, she didn't. She just hung her head in her hands and started to cry again.

I stood and watched her for a moment. I figured I had two choices. I could either walk away, feeling empowered because I had made the school tough-nut cry, or I could offer her the hand of friendship it looked like she needed. I dug into the side pocket of my bag and pulled out the packet of Kleenex Mum always made me carry.

I went over to her and sat back down. By this time she was really sobbing. I gave her a tissue and tentatively put my arm around her shoulders to reassure her, and I myself was reassured when she didn't shrug it away.

'What's the matter?' I asked gently. 'Is there anything I can do?' She shook her head and tried to speak, but all that came out was a weird strangulated gasp. We sat there for a while, until eventually she was calm enough to speak.

'You know my brother Ben's a fireman?' she snuffled.

I nodded and encouraged her to continue. 'He was involved in a really bad accident yesterday.'

'God, I'm so sorry,' I said, and really meant it. 'Is he okay?' I was half expecting her to tell me he'd been killed. She started crying some more and I braced myself for the worst. 'He is,' she sniffed, nodding. 'But one of his mates died.'

'Blimey,' I said. 'That sucks. Did you know him well?' I figured she must have done to be this upset. She shook her head; she didn't know him at all. This left me puzzled. I mean, yeah, it was terrible and all that, but why was she in such a state?

'It could have been him,' she said, her cheeks red and shiny. 'What would I have done if it was him?' she wailed, getting upset all over again.

'Hey, it wasn't him,' I soothed, as I stroked her strawberry blonde ringlets. 'He's fine and you don't have to worry.' I was aware it sounded like lip service, but I didn't want to think about it too much. I didn't want to tell her I'd lost a sibling; at least, not yet.

'I know stuff like this is horrible and it makes you feel all edgy, but if anything, it's just going to make them all a lot more careful now, isn't it? I mean, whenever there's a car crash, people drive around like pensioners, don't they?' I hoped this would help her get it into perspective. It seemed to, as she smiled at me gratefully, and I realized that the ice was well and truly broken.

We stayed there for a while, chatting while she dabbed at her eyes and touched up her make-up. I borrowed a bit just to keep her company. We turned up late to registration. Mr Bennet just raised his eyes and didn't even bother to ask us for an excuse.

'Where've you two been?' asked Zara as we sat down.

'Just chatting,' said Abby, smiling at me.

'So where's Steph, then?' asked Zara again. We both looked at her empty seat and shrugged. She'd been missing a lot lately, since she'd started going out with Gavin in year twelve.

The bell rang for morning lessons and we all got our books out for double Maths. Yuk. As we scraped our chairs back and stood up, Mr Bennet held his hands in the air and shushed us. He picked up a pile of white forms from his desk and my heart sank. Not another trip I wouldn't be allowed to go on.

'These are consent forms,' he announced, handing them to Heidi to give out. 'I'd like you all to take them home and get them signed by Friday.'

'What are they for, Sir?' asked Zara, winking at Abby. She knew full well it was for the dreaded sex talk. Mr Bennet astutely ignored her and I noticed across the room that Brian flushed a little. It made me like him even more that he got embarrassed about stuff like that.

Suddenly the door flung open and a breathless Steph came running into the room.

'Sorry I'm late,' she panted to Mr Bennet as she came and sat beside me.

'Late night?' probed Zara knowingly.

'Wouldn't you like to know?' replied Steph, grinning from ear to ear.

FOUR

After what happened on the History trip, I realized it was a bad idea to keep stuff from my dad. I also worked out from my other brother, Lee, that if you want something from him, don't ask until he's on at least his second can of beer.

Dad had his feet up on the table, watching football, when I came down from my room with the form. I had a speech already prepared. I wasn't going to lie; I just wasn't going to go into too much detail about what the lesson would be about. I sat on the arm of the sofa, helping myself to a handful of his crisps and pretending I was really interested in the match. I opened my mouth, just about to ask him, when the doorbell went. Typical.

'I'll get it,' I sang, hoping being cheerful around him might help with my cause. When I opened the door, my heart sank into my shoes. Lee was standing there, flanked by two policemen.

'Your mum or dad around?' one of them asked.

'Yeah,' I murmured. 'Hang on.' I went back into the lounge, bracing myself for fireworks.

'Dad?' I said, as gently as I could. No reply. 'Dad?' I said, a little louder.

'What?' he growled, leaning forward to study the replay. I took a deep breath and told him about the policeman at the door. He, too, took a deep breath, muttering, 'What's the little tyke done now?' to himself as he headed out to the porch.

Lee's always getting into trouble, even now. It's not that he's a bad person. He says it's 'cos he gets bored easily and can't stop himself from fiddling. Even as a kid he was always dismantling his toys then helping himself to mine when he couldn't put them back together.

This time, he'd been caught tying some elastic across a road between two lampposts. 'Just to see what happened,' was his defence. He's actually a year older than me, but you'd never know, as he's so immature. I felt really annoyed with him that night. It was Thursday and I had to get the form back to Mr Bennet the next day, and there was no way I was going to risk faking my dad's signature again.

Dad yelled at Lee and Lee yelled at Dad for ages. I tried drowning it out with my music, but then I got yelled at by both of them. In the end, I think Lee must have stormed off somewhere as I heard the front door go. He does that sometimes when he can't hack Dad. He's even not come home a few nights.

I waited up until midnight, when I was sure Dad would have fallen asleep in front of the telly. I crept downstairs as quietly as I could and peered in on him. He was snoring. With the form in my hand, I gently woke him up and told him to go to bed. He seemed disorientated and kept blinking so his eyes would get accustomed to the light.

'What time is it?' His voice was thick and slow with sleep.

'Late,' I said as he headed out of the room. I jumped ahead of him to open the door and as casually as I could told him we were having a sex talk at school and that I needed his signature to let the school know he was okay with it.

'What sort of things are they going to talk to you about?' he asked suspiciously.

'I don't know,' I said. 'I'm not psychic.' He grunted and read the form through fuzzy eyes, scratching his excuse for a signature at the bottom with a pen I just happened to have ready. He kissed me clumsily, reminded me to turn everything off, and then heavily made his way up the stairs, using the banister as a winch.

***

I felt apprehensive on the day of the sex talk. It's not that I didn't already know about stuff like STIs and blow-jobs; it's just that hearing Miss Jennings discuss it so frankly and mechanically made me want to giggle. I'm always the same in situations that call for straight-faced order. They make me nervous.

Luckily for us, the boys were separated from the girls while we had the *'Girls And Their World'* talk. It was a bit late for all the period stuff 'cos most of us had started yonks ago, except maybe Jane, but apparently her sister was seventeen before it happened.

The talk was mostly boring, until we played this really stupid game. Miss Jennings had a massive poster of the female body, some names of the various reproductive bits and some pins. We had to split into groups and work out where they all went.

Steph deliberately got all hers wrong, and made us all nearly wet ourselves by sticking an ovary on the ear and a fallopian tube on the wrist. Of course, Miss Jennings wasn't remotely amused and she scowled at us until the juice and biscuits at half-time.

After the break, we all had to file into the hall with the boys and watch a cartoon film about safe sex. I was glad it was dark in there, as I was sure I'd gone red. Zara and Brian were sitting in front of me. I saw her edge closer to him and put her hand on his thigh, rubbing it gently. I wondered if they'd done it yet, then felt sick when I got a visual image.

The lights came flickering on and Miss Jennings and Mr Lawrence, head of P.E., asked if anyone had any questions. A few of the boys asked really stupid stuff to get a laugh from their mates. When it was clear no one was going to ask anything sensible, we got handed loads of leaflets and a three-pack of condoms each, and finally the torture was over.

With ten minutes to go before the next lesson, all the girls gathered in the cloakroom to analyse and discuss, and of course have a good look at our freebies.

'You are using these, aren't you?' asked Zara, waving her box of condoms at Steph.

'Doh, 'course we are. We're not stupid,' said Steph. She might not be, but I certainly wouldn't trust Gavin Carter to put his socks on properly, let alone anything as technical as a condom.

'Come on, let's open one,' said Abby, grabbing Zara's box from her hand.

'Oi, use your own,' screeched Zara as she snatched them back.

'What's your problem? They'll be out of date by the time you need them,' said Abby in a sarky tone.

'Here, have mine,' I said, thrusting them at her. There was no way I'd be needing them any time soon, and I could tell Zara was getting annoyed by all the teasing about her and Brian not having done it yet.

Abby peeled the cellophane off the box with relish, and we all crowded round. She opened the box and pulled out the foil-wrapped johnnie.

'Eurgh!' she exclaimed, pressing it in her fingers. 'I can feel it sliming around in there. Have a go,' she said, handing it to Zara.

'Eurgh!' echoed Zara, ripping the top of the wrapping. She nudged me and I reluctantly held a palm out, ready to catch it as she squeezed it out. It plopped into my palm like a slimy fish. It looked like a cross between an elastic band and the teat of a doll's bottle I had when I was a kid.

'Unroll it then!' urged Steph impatiently. I didn't want to touch it; it smelled funny. Abby reached over and grabbed it out of my hand. Pinching the tip in her fingers, she slowly unravelled it, all of us giggling, but unable to take our eyes off it.

She held it aloft so we could all have a good look, then suddenly threw it in my face, making me gasp. The others laughed as I stuffed it down Zara's jumper. She wriggled to get it free and chased me round the locker room with it. I saw Steph raise her eyes at Abby. I think she thought we were being immature, but I didn't care; it was fun.

When we sat back down again, Zara pulled out the leaflet that came in the box and started laughing at the dodgy drawings of men with erections. Still acting a bit aloof, Abby took the opportunity to quiz Steph on exactly how far she'd gone with Gavin. Steph played it coy at first but I could tell she couldn't wait to spill the beans.

'So ...?' urged Abby. 'What was it like?'

'Amazing,' she said, closing her eyes and shuddering as she remembered.

'He doesn't look like he's amazing in bed,' said Zara, looking miffed. I had to agree with her. I don't think I'd ever actually heard Gavin speak; he just kind of grunted at people. He'd looked totally ridiculous since he got his mum to cut his hair like David Beckham's with her Ladyshave.

'What would you know?' sneered Steph. 'It's not as if you and Brian do anything but hold hands, is it?'

'We do stuff!' retorted Zara angrily.

'Yeah, but going to church doesn't count,' sniggered Abby.

'Is Brian religious?' I asked Zara, surprised.

'So what if he is?'

'Nothing,' I said. 'I think it's pretty cool, actually.'

'You would, wouldn't you, little miss freaky mouse,' said Steph. The others laughed, but I was stung. Was that really what she thought of me? I was quiet for a while as they continued to talk. I watched with morbid curiosity as Abby peeled a sample of moisturizer from the pages of a magazine and squeezed its contents into the condom. She tied a knot in it and Steph assured her it looked like an authentic used one. Everyone laughed and it was thrown around the room again.

'So come on then,' probed Abby looking at me with a smirk. 'How far have you gone?'

I shrugged. All I'd actually done was snog one of Lee's friends with tongues last summer, but I wasn't about to tell them that. Thinking on my feet, I made up a story about him feeling my boobs. I told them we would have gone further if we hadn't been disturbed, but even so, they weren't impressed.

I felt uncomfortable and Zara must have sensed it.

'Leave her alone,' she warned Abby and Steph. 'Just 'cos we're not all dirty slags like you two,' she joked.

'That's not what you told me,' said Abby, stirring. Zara glared at her. It was obviously meant to be a secret. Abby ignored her. 'Didn't you tell me you did it with that Paul bloke at Christmas?' she said, pretending to sound confused, so Zara would be forced to explain.

'I did,' Zara said, looking uncomfortable. 'But it was ages ago and he was crap.'

'Didn't you have an O?' asked Steph with mock sympathy.

''Course not, you never do the first time,' replied Zara knowingly. We all looked at Steph. She was the only one qualified to confirm or deny.

'Poor you,' she said. 'I had three.'

With that, everyone whooped and laughed, but I felt a bit sorry for Zara – she looked dead embarrassed.

FIVE

I was a bit grumpy when I got home. I felt like I was the only virgin in school. I mean, Abby was too, but she'd done loads more than me and with more than one person. I made a mental note to get more experience as soon as was humanly possible. But how could I when I didn't fancy anyone? Well, there was one person I fancied, but Brian very definitely belonged to Zara.

She called me after tea and I was glad 'cos it meant Lee had to do all the washing up on his own. I took the portable phone into my room and told her about my concerns. She said she'd have a think about which boys in our year would be suitable and that she'd try to fix me up. I asked if Brian had any decent friends, thinking that if I couldn't have him then someone like him would be good enough.

We talked more about how experienced everyone in our year was, and then Zara went a bit quiet and distant. I thought she must be bored 'cos I was talking about this really hot boy at my old school. I asked her if she wanted to go, and she said she had a secret. She made me swear not to tell Steph or Abby. I promised and she revealed that she didn't exactly do it with Paul; in fact, she didn't get anywhere near.

I told her it didn't bother me and I kind of liked the fact we had one more thing in common. I told her that she shouldn't feel under pressure to lie about having sex. I'd just started telling her that in America, loads of kids think it's really cool to still be a virgin, when there was a click on the line.

'I'm on the phone,' I said.

'Well, get off it,' came my dad's gruff reply. The phone clicked again as he put the extension in the lounge down.

'Is he always such a miserable bugger?' asked Zara.

'Pretty much,' I laughed. 'See you tomorrow.' We said goodbye and hung up. Within seconds Dad was calling me. 'I'm off!' I yelled, thinking he still thought I was on the phone. Mum always rang at eight when she was away and it was three minutes to.

'Get down here, now!' he yelled back at me.

'Oh, God,' I sighed. What had I done now?

I got off my bed and went downstairs, racking my brain for any chores I hadn't done around the house. Dad was sitting by the computer. I thought I must have forgotten to log off when I checked my e-mails. It's one of Dad's pet hates.

'I'm not angry,' he said, sounding angry. 'I just want to know who you're sleeping with.'

Behind him, Lee raised his eyes and shook his finger in a 'you are dead meat' kind of way. He stood there, arms crossed, mirroring Dad and grinning as he waited to see how I was going to get out of this one.

'What are you on about?' I wondered if he had heard more of my phone conversation with Zara than I'd thought.

'I found these in your bag,' he said, holding up the opened box of condoms. I didn't know what to say. For a start I was furious that he'd been going through my things. I also knew I shouldn't have kept them.

'There's one missing,' added Lee helpfully.

'Lee, scram! This is nothing to do with you.' Lee shrugged. He really wasn't that bothered. If Dad was having a go at me, then at least he was off Lee's case; so off he went, out somewhere in search of a different kind of amusement.

'This!' Dad shouted, shaking the box at me, '... was not all I found in there.' He took a deep breath. I hadn't seen him this wound-up in ages. 'I never thought I'd hear myself say this ... but you disgust me!' I was dumbstruck. What else was there in my bag and why was he so angry?

'So come on then, who is he?'

'Nobody.'

He tutted before I could finish my sentence. 'What's your mother going to say?' I looked at the floor. He obviously didn't believe me. 'Don't you think we've got enough going on at the moment?'

'We got them free at the sex-talk lesson today.' He looked at me blankly. 'Don't you remember you signed the form to say it was okay last week?' I prompted hopefully.

'I signed a form saying it was okay for you to be educated about this stuff, not encouraged to go out there and do it at the first chance you get.'

'Dad, just 'cos I have some condoms, it doesn't automatically mean I'm having sex.'

'Don't lie to me, Lisa,' he shouted. 'You're in more than enough trouble already!'

I sighed. How was I meant to win? It was so far from the truth it was laughable.

'But even if I had, at least I'd have been careful.'

'Don't get clever with me. Nobody likes a slut!' He looked me up and down with disgust. 'I'll be talking to your teacher about this.' Great, I thought, my heart sinking. I hadn't got over the last embarrassment yet.

* * *

Unable to be in the same house as his evil daughter, Dad went straight to the pub without even waiting in for Mum to call. I was still rooted to the spot where Dad had left me, trying to make sense of the accusations and work out a way to prove I wasn't lying when the phone rang.

Mum was annoyed Dad wasn't around, especially when I told her where he was. I probably shouldn't have done, but I was angry and wanted to get back at him. She sounded tired and a bit down in the dumps. Ordinarily I would have talked to her more, but I was preoccupied and upset. After assuring her there was no news and everyone was fine, she got the message and said she'd better go and hand some more leaflets out.

She sounded sad as she hung up and I got a pang of guilt that maybe I should have talked to her more about what was going on over there. The thing is that every time she went away, I got upset. I missed her, but I was annoyed with her at the same time for not being with me. Yeah, I know. It sounds crazy, doesn't it?

Anyway, I grabbed my bag off the table and went up to my room. I didn't feel much like homework. I didn't feel much like anything. I put some music on and sat on the bed, still upset by the injustice of my dad's tirade. Annoyed and wanting to find out what had upset him so much, I grabbed my school bag and tipped everything onto my bed.

I sifted through my pencil-case, calculator, purse, homework books and mobile, examining them all before putting them back into the bag. I was growing more and more confused. I knew my dad was under pressure having to find new premises for the garage, but was he losing it?

But then I saw it, sticking to the cover of my mini-atlas, the unmistakeable fake used condom. Thanks, Abby. My heart sank into my shoes as I understood why Dad went so mad. From my limited knowledge of these things, I had to admit, it did look pretty real.

SIX

'So, did you like your er … present?' Abby asked, trying to look innocent as we queued for our lunch.

'Yeah, ha ha, very funny,' I said. I didn't know what time Dad had got back from the pub the night before, but it was way after I went to bed and he'd left already when I got up. Lee reckoned he was so disappointed with me he couldn't even be at the same breakfast table. I couldn't even be bothered to tell him the truth. He wouldn't have believed me anyway.

'What's the matter? Can't you take a joke?' Steph leaned across me for a bread roll.

'Yeah I can …' I said. 'But my Dad can't.'

'He didn't find it?' asked Abby dramatically, not daring to believe something this juicy could be true.

'Yeah, he did. He went ballistic and now he won't talk to me, thanks to you two.' They looked at each other and exploded into laughter. They were impressed with their handiwork and the headache at home it had given me.

'You've got to see the funny side,' said Steph, as we took our trays over to an empty table. 'Your Dad'll calm down about it … in a few years.' They both laughed even harder and I felt miserable. Zara had managed to blag the morning off for an orthodontist appointment. I was missing her. She was pretty good at protecting me from these two. We ate lunch in silence.

I was pleased when Brian came over to join us. He wanted to know what time Zara would be turning up.

'Why don't you wait with us?' I suggested, shuffling along the bench. 'She won't be long.' He put his tray down and sat next to me. There were empty spaces by both Steph and Abby, but he didn't sit next to them, he sat next to me. Although I enjoyed the proximity, I couldn't look at him without turning my whole head and making it totally obvious. I sneaked a few peeps out of the corner of my eye, but had to be careful. This was the kind of thing Steph and Abby would pounce on if they cottoned on to it.

'So …' said Steph, as she watched him eat, 'Zara's a per-etty frustrated lady, if you know what I mean. Any plans to put her out of her misery?' Abby giggled. It didn't take much to set her off. I blushed. I knew what it was like to be put on the spot by Steph. But then at the same time, I was anxious for him to reply.

'Thought I might take her to see Urban Strawberry Lunch at the weekend,' he said coolly, not rising to the bait. None of us had the faintest idea what he was talking about. He must have worked this out from the looks on our faces, and he seemed amused.

'Well?' prompted Steph, a little riled she hadn't managed to get to him.

'It's this travelling group,' he explained. 'They have these massive drums made out of bins and barrels, and loads of sticks and stuff. They set up in the town centre at lunchtime and get stressed-out office people to come and have a bang with them.'

'Kinky!' said Abby. 'I knew you were a randy little git underneath all that God-squad rubbish.'

'Grow up, Abby.' A little girl inside me applauded him wildly for being brave enough to say this. 'It's to relieve tension. Makes you feel loads better if you're a bit hacked off about stuff.'

'I could do with that,' I said, thinking of all the hassles at home.

'What are you stressed out about?' he asked, genuinely concerned … I think.

'Oh, nothing.' I tried to brush it aside.

'Her dad chucked a mental 'cos he found a used john-nie in her bag,' said Abby. Brian looked at me with a glim-mer of incredulity. I also saw a slight grimace.

'It wasn't real; they played a trick on me,' I corrected quickly. But was it too late?

***

It got too hot in the canteen and it stank of overcooked food. We took our drinks and went to sit outside, behind the pool. I'd wanted to stay and talk to Brian more about Urban Strawberry Lunch, but Steph and Abby wanted me to help them come up with a plan to persuade Abby's dad to let Steph stay for the summer.

We lay on our fronts, trying to think of a solution. My heart wasn't really in it and I gave up after the second of my ideas was pooh-poohed. I flipped over, rolled up my sleeves and closed my eyes, enjoying the hot sun on my skin and the smell of freshly cut grass. Steph and Abby's voices became distant and I had a nice daydream about Brian.

I must have nodded off as the next thing I knew, some-one was sprinkling grass over my face. I sat up, blinking, and saw it was Abby.

'I'm bored.'

'Where's Steph?' I asked, looking around and picking a bit of grass out of my mouth.

'Gone off somewhere with Gavin,' she moaned. 'I bet they're shagging.'

'Is that *all* they do?' I asked.

'Seems like it. I hate the way she just drops her friends whenever he's around. All he has to do is click his fingers and she goes running.' I felt a bit sorry for her; sometimes you do just want a best friend all to yourself. Her face brightened when Zara appeared.

'All right, skiver?' said Abby. 'How did it go?'

'Fantastic!' she said, grinning. Neither of us could guess how a trip to the dentist could have made her that happy.

'Okay …' said Abby, bemused by Zara's odd behaviour. 'Own up. Who nicked the miserable, moaning Zara and put this alien in her place?' We all laughed.

'What's going on?' I asked her. She looked around to make sure no one else could hear. She put her hand in her school bag and pulled out a set of keys, dangling them above all of us.

'Who's up for a party?' she said with relish.

While having lunch in the café, her dad had happened to let slip that his chef was away on holiday and he was keeping an eye on his house. Zara had done what all the teachers are always telling us to do and seized the day, as well as the chef's house keys while her dad wasn't looking.

* * *

The excitement didn't last for long. Steph was in a right mood when she got back from her liaison with Gavin. He'd told her he thought they should have a break; he didn't want to be tied down to just one person at his age. Steph was livid. She'd never been dumped before. Personally, I took the news with dread. If Steph's life wasn't going well, then no one else's was allowed to.

That afternoon, some of the lads in our class persuaded Mr Baines, our Biology teacher, to let us have the lesson outside, as it was so hot. They'd been trying it on with all the other teachers all week to no avail, so we were surprised when he agreed, but then he was new and didn't know any better.

We were separated into groups on the playing field. Each group had to take a square metre of grass and log how many types of grass, insects and soil we could find. We went as far away from Mr Baines and the rest of the class as possible and sat down, half-heartedly digging as we did our best to console Steph.

'He's not worth it,' offered Zara, doodling on her clip-board. I suspected she was annoyed that Steph was in such a strop when all she wanted to do was organize her party.

'Yeah,' added Abby. 'If he can't appreciate how great you are, then he doesn't deserve you.' Steph just carried on staring at the ground and picking at the soil. We all looked at each other, none of us knowing what to do.

'I really hate him,' Steph said suddenly.

'He's a git,' I offered, without thinking, but I really did think he was. Steph smiled at me oddly, then started to laugh.

'Yeah, he is,' she agreed. 'A great big, fat, stinking git,' she giggled.

'A great big, fat, stinking git with a small willy?' suggested Abby.

'Yep, a great big, fat, stinking git with a small willy and bad breath,' said Steph, starting to really enjoy herself.

'And a dodgy haircut,' added Zara. We all nodded as we started laughing.

'A *very* dodgy haircut,' said Steph, suddenly feeling loads better. Our gaggle of giggles alerted Mr Baines to the fact that not much work was getting done in our corner of the field. He came over and asked us what we had discovered. We all got a detention when he saw our blank worksheets.

SEVEN

A few nights later, laden with booze nicked from our parents, the four of us let ourselves into the house to get it ready for the party. Zara was planning to seduce Brian, so went straight upstairs to suss out the bedroom situation, taking Steph with her for advice. Abby and I put our stuff down and had a nose around. It was big, very big, and in one of the kitchen cupboards we found a few bottles of spirits.

'Ever made punch?' Abby asked me. I shook my head. I'd never even tasted it.

'It can't be that hard,' she said, thinking out loud as she examined the labels on the bottles. We couldn't find a bowl big enough, so we rinsed out a bucket and used that. At first, we just put a taster from a few bottles in with loads of lemonade and orange juice, but it didn't really taste of anything other than Orangina past its sell-by date.

I put a CD on to get us in the mood and Abby got more adventurous and started adding huge glugs from nearly all the bottles as she swung her hips and sang her head off. By the time she'd finished, the concoction was so strong it could have singed your nose hairs. We'd run out of lemonade and there was only half a carton of orange juice left. I looked for something else to dilute it a bit, but all I could find was Ribena. We made up a couple of pints with water and chucked them in. Suddenly it tasted lush.

Steph and Zara had been gone ages, so we decided to go and look for them. We found them sitting on the bed, chatting, in a really cool room right at the back of the house. It was painted deep purple and had posters over the ceiling.

'Doesn't look much like a chef lives here,' commented Abby, as she nosed around at other stuff in the room.

'He's a landlord as well,' explained Zara. 'He rents these rooms out to students.' Suddenly we all felt really cool to be having a house party in a proper student house.

'Shall I go and get us all some punch?' I offered, feeling really excited. Everyone nodded eagerly and I raced downstairs, not wanting to miss anything.

When I came back into the room, clutching four mugs of our concoction, Zara was pulling the curtains and putting the lights down low. She took some tea lights out of a carrier bag, lit them with a handy box of matches nearby, and scattered them around the room. She also took out some make-up, some sexy underwear she'd nicked from her sister and her three-pack of condoms.

'Where shall I put these?' she asked Steph. 'I don't want it to look too set-up.'

'If he was a normal teenage boy, he'd have been carrying his own since he was three,' answered Steph dryly. 'But seeing as this is Brian we're talking about, he might need a bit of a helping hand.' She stood up and looked around the room, considering.

'Under the pillow's probably best. Out of sight but easy access.' She looked pleased with herself. Next, she looked Zara up and down. 'You're not wearing that, are you?'

'No way. This,' she said, pulling a really cool top out of her carrier bag. We'd all brought a change of clothes, so the next half an hour was spent getting tarted up and borrowing each other's make-up. Just as Abby was wriggling into her dress, Steph was helping Zara do her top up and I was applying lip-gloss, the doorbell rang. We all looked at each other and squealed with excitement.

As I was the closest to being ready, I went downstairs to let the boys in, turning the music up a notch as I went. When I opened the door, Brian and the rest of his band were standing there. Not only had they brought beer and cider, but all their instruments as well. I heard Zara coming down the stairs as I let them in. She gave Brian a very special smile.

'Why have you brought all your gear?' she asked, after delivering a saucy kiss.

'Thought we could have a quick practice while we're here,' he said, taking his jacket off.

'Cool,' I said. Zara flashed a look at me and I realized I'd said the wrong thing. There was only one thing on her mind that night, and it wasn't band practice.

***

Brian's band, The Seventh Order, turned out to be pretty good. In fact, I was disappointed when Zara ceremoniously pulled the power cable from the amp. She took Brian by the hand and, without speaking, led him upstairs. I felt a bit funny, knowing what they were up to, so decided to get some more punch. When I got back, the bass player, a lad called Mark, had gone to the loo, so I helped myself to his bass.

I used to love music when I was a kid. I would have done it for GCSE, but Dad didn't want me to take it as one of my options. I sat there plucking away, making up a tune. It took my mind off what was going on all around me. Abby and Steph were playing drinking games with Jamie and Noel. They all seemed pretty out of it.

Mark came back and seemed worried at first that I was going to break his bass. I promised him I'd be gentle. I just liked the feel of it in my hands; I liked the way the strings dug into my fingers, leaving little red grooves behind.

After a while, and a few more cans of beer, Mark seemed to relax. He said I was pretty good and showed me a few more difficult notes. He sat behind me, with his hands on mine, and I liked it. I felt safe with him all around me and he smelled good, too. I'd never really had a good look at him before, but he was really cute. He had brown eyes, not as dark as Brian's, and a mop of tousled hazelnut-coloured hair.

While he was looking down, his head a few inches from mine, I had an urge to kiss him and so I did, just a peck on the cheek, nothing major. The punch must have made me brave or something, 'cos I never do stuff like that. He stopped playing and looked at me. It was such an intense moment. I felt his hands tighten around mine on the bass and he leaned a little closer. In the corner of my eye, I could see Abby nudging Steph and pointing at me, but I didn't care. Mark was going to kiss me.

'Woo-woo,' one of them whistled, breaking the magical moment.

'She's a dark horse, that one,' teased Steph. It was one of those moments when you really wish your friends would disappear.

'Oi, you two,' shouted Steph, 'there's enough of that malarkey going on upstairs.' She grabbed two more cushions off the sofa and patted them. 'Come on, let's play spin the bottle.' I was quite happy where I was and I'm pretty sure Mark was, too, but Steph is one of those girls you just can't say no to. Reluctantly, we went over and joined in. I felt anxious. I'd never played the game before and didn't want to make a fool of myself in front of Mark.

I held my breath when it was my turn to spin. My stomach was doing back-flips and my heart was beating too fast. I drank more punch as I waited for the bottle to stop, but it seemed to take forever. I was gutted when it landed on Abby, but relieved it wasn't Jamie or Noel.

'Eurgh! There's no way you're snogging me,' she said, reaching a hand out and grabbing the bottle. She moved it a little to the left until it pointed directly at Mark. 'Everyone happy if Mark takes my place?' she asked. Steph grinned in anticipation.

'Sure you don't want to give us some lesbo love action?' teased Noel hopefully. Abby answered him with a sarky smile. I looked at Mark and he looked at me. I didn't want to make the first move, not in front of everybody.

'Well, are you going to do it or have a forfeit?' prompted an impatient Steph. I looked at Mark again and he shrugged nonchalantly, shuffling a little closer and leaning towards me. I followed suit and closed my eyes as we kissed to a round of applause from the others. It didn't last long and it wasn't great. His lips were a bit rough and we were both tense. I really wanted him to make me feel how Brian did, but the truth was, he came nowhere near.

I pulled away, trying to mask my disappointment, and Steph took her turn. I looked up to see Brian coming down the stairs. He didn't look happy. Suddenly and stupidly I felt guilty, as if by kissing Mark I had betrayed him. He didn't say a word, just went into the kitchen and got another beer from the fridge. We heard it snap open.

When he hadn't come back into the lounge after five minutes and Zara hadn't come downstairs either, we all started looking at each other, wondering what was up. The whole world knew about Zara's plan, but no one knew why it had seemingly fallen apart. I tried to hide my secret pleasure. Maybe Brian was in love with me after all?

Eventually, Steph went upstairs to see if Zara was all right. I went into the kitchen on the pretext of getting more drinks. Brian looked really narky and just mumbled when I asked him if he was okay. I got the impression that he wanted to be alone, so just filled my mug with punch and went back to the game. The more I drank, the more fun I had. I tried to reassure myself that if Brian was going to be off with me, then I'd just have a good time with Mark.

Steph finally came back downstairs with a tear-stained Zara in tow. She whispered to me and Abby that Brian had told her he didn't want to do it, so now she thought he didn't love her. She told us to give her a few drinks and include her in the game while she went and had a chat with Brian. If anyone could sort this out, she could, or so she said.

We all tried our best to cheer Zara up. We turned the music up to the max and dragged her up to dance with us. She did, half-heartedly, before slumping back down onto the sofa and looking miserable. In the end, feeling quite queasy by this stage, we too slumped down either side of her and a drunken silence fell on the room. No one had the energy to change the CD.

The boys communed in the kitchen, where the booze was, and we stayed where we were for ages. Zara's mood had brought the whole party crashing down. After a while, Steph came downstairs.

'How's it going?' asked Zara.

'Pretty good, I think,' said Steph.

'Can I go up there yet?'

'In a bit. I think I've got him to change his mind. One more drink should relax him enough.' With that, she had disappeared into the kitchen, ruling out the possibility of any more small talk. I could tell that Zara felt helpless and even more miserable than before.

'I don't even think I want to do it any more,' she said after Steph had gone back upstairs again. 'I mean, he obviously doesn't find me sexy or he'd have jumped on me when he had the chance.' She was frank and, in retrospect, she was probably right.

'Of course he fancies you, or he wouldn't be your boyfriend,' I said. I could tell Zara wasn't that convinced, but she couldn't be bothered to argue the point. I think, like the rest of us, she was sick of talking about it.

When the beer had dried up and Steph and Brian still hadn't reappeared, Mark came back into the lounge to tell us he and the lads were going to hit the road. If he'd said that a few hours before, I might have cared, but as things were I couldn't decide whether I wanted to puke my guts up or go to sleep.

'Do you think I should go up there?' asked Zara.

'Maybe,' I said, trying to keep my eyes open.

'Will you come with me?' she asked Abby. Abby nodded and they stood up.

'Hey, don't leave me down here on my own,' I said.

'So come with us,' said Zara from halfway up the stairs.

I don't know why, but we tip-toed along the landing. Something about the darkness and the closed doors called for it. We stopped outside the purple bedroom and Zara pressed her ear to the door.

'I can't hear anything,' she whispered after a few moments. 'Shall I go in?' We both shrugged. Zara seemed oblivious to what we were thinking, but as I caught Abby's eye, I knew she didn't like the look of this either.

'I bet they've fallen asleep,' she said, turning the handle. 'Thanks a lot, Steph,' she added sarcastically as she walked into the room. It took us all a few moments for our eyes to get used to the dim candlelight, but we knew even before we saw it why Zara had frozen on the spot. Abby flicked the light switch and there they were, Brian and Steph, butt-naked, writhing around under the covers.

No one spoke. Brian and Steph tried to cover them-selves up, Zara started to cry, Abby just stood there with her gob hanging open, and I felt sick, really sick. Zara ran out of the room and downstairs. I went straight to the bathroom and threw up. I think Abby might have stayed rooted to the spot until Brian asked her to leave so he could get dressed.

As soon as I felt well enough, I went downstairs. I found Abby consoling a sobbing Zara in the garden. Brian came out to try to talk to her, and she ended up pummelling his chest until we pulled her off.

'I'm so sorry,' he said. 'I don't know how it happened.'

'Just go, Brian,' said Abby dismissively with her arm around Zara. 'Can't you see she doesn't want to talk to you?' I looked at him and wanted to hit him myself, I was so disappointed. I mean, I know I didn't want him to sleep with Zara, but I'd rather her than Steph. Steph didn't care about him; she was just using him.

He looked at me, as I was the only one acknowledging his existence. 'I'm sorry,' he said again.

'What are you saying it to me for?' I shouted. He seemed shocked by my anger and I remember feeling pleased. As he turned to go, we heard the front door slam. We were all too drunk and emotional to work out what was going on. That is, until the chef walked in. He looked around his messy, beer-stained home, and then saw us all in the garden, none of us in any state to be quick-witted enough to hide.

'What the hell are you lot doing in my house?'

Zara started crying again.

EIGHT

I can't tell you how much trouble we all got in for that. Steph's summer staying with Abby lasted just three days. When Mr Davies found out, he packed her off to her parents on the first train and Abby had to go and stay with her mum in Cornwall for two weeks. That left me, and of course Zara who, understandably, was mortified by Brian's infidelity.

Her mum had got her a job working in the local dry-cleaning shop, so I didn't see that much of her. I proba-bly couldn't have done anyway, even if shc'd been around, as things were getting really hairy at home.

It started when Mum got back from her trip to Ibiza. She always came back exhausted and depressed. Dad never knew what to do or what to say, so inevitably ended up saying the wrong thing and before you know it, World War Three had broken out. None of it was helped by Lee. He chose to be a total pain in the bum and drove us all crazy with his stupid, selfish ways.

I can't remember if I told you, but my brother Dan is really into rally driving. He's got his own car and every-thing. One day, Lee had the hump. He'd been going on and on about a scooter he'd seen that he was saving up for. He kept nagging Mum and Dad to buy it for him, which I thought was pretty selfish, seeing as Mum was having to do two jobs to make ends meet.

Anyway, Mum wasn't in the mood to discuss it, so she sent him out to look for a job. He'd just done his GCSEs and was adamant there was no way he was going back to school or college or anything; he'd had it with education. At the same time, though, he didn't want a job and didn't see why he should have to get one. He wanted to enjoy his summer, go wild, have an adventure.

It was teatime when the police brought him home. He'd nicked Dan's rally car and crashed it, and it was two weeks before a big race as well. Dan grabbed him by the neck. I've never seen him so angry in my life. If Mum and Dad hadn't stepped in, I really think he would have killed Lee. He certainly didn't look like he was messing.

None of us noticed Mum crying while Dad was dealing with the boys. I was trying to keep as low a profile as possible after the party fiasco. It started out with her shaking. She almost looked like she was laughing. Then she made this awful noise as she gasped for air and started sobbing, and by that I mean really crying, like a baby. Everyone was so shocked they stopped fighting, and for ages we all stood and stared at her, not really knowing what to do.

Dad rushed over and put his arms around her.

'See what you've done?' he glared at Lee. 'You've upset your mother.'

'It wasn't just me,' whined Lee 'What about him?' he demanded, thumbing Dan.

'Shh,' I hissed at him as I went and sat on the other side of Mum.

'Come on love, we've stopped rowing now,' said Dad, worry lines burrowed across his face.

'It's not that,' she wailed '… I miss her.' She clenched her fists and banged them against her chest. 'I miss her so much.' And then I started crying.

You see, the thing is, I've got an older sister, Ellie. She went missing when I was fourteen. She went on holiday to Ibiza and never came back. She never called, never wrote, never spent any money from her bank account; she just disappeared off the face of the earth. At first, we were convinced she'd turn up, but as time went by, it became harder and harder to believe that she'd hurt us that way by not getting in touch. It was the only thing that made sense, but none of us was willing to believe that she was dead.

***

Mum and Dad stayed up talking about Ellie late into the night. I heard them both crying at one stage and it made my chest tight and horrible. I didn't sleep well at all. I kept waking up and checking the clock, listening out for the silence that meant Mum and Dad had finally gone to bed. At one stage, I could hear them in their bedroom, but they weren't asleep. The slow, heavy murmurings of their grief still carried through the night air and I felt angry with them for reminding me. I could only cope with Ellie being gone as long as I pushed it to the back of my mind and left it there.

In the end I gave up trying to sleep. I just lay there in the dark wondering what Ellie was doing, where she was, who she was with. The scary thoughts soon rushed in as they often did at night, mostly in my dreams. I couldn't help but imagine her being raped and murdered and buried somewhere that we'd never find her. You see horrific stuff like that on the news the whole time. Why should my family have a happy ending?

My earliest memory of Ellie was when I was four and she was seven. Mum and Dad used to take us to Tenby every summer in the caravan. We never had much money, but we always had a good time and got treated to fish and chips eaten straight from the paper on the beach on our last day.

It was a baking hot summer and we had the best of it the week we were there that year. Mum sat on the beach with us, too busy to help with our sandcastle town, as she had a lot of reading to do. She was just about to do a teacher-training course. Dad had taken Dan and Lee fishing further up the coast.

Ellie had made friends with a girl called Sarah at the caravan park. She had a rubber dinghy and one day when she was going to a museum with her parents, she let Ellie borrow it. It was beautiful, bright red with a blue stripe. It took Ellie an hour to blow it up. She'd forgotten to ask for the foot pump. I remember getting impatient and sulky about having to wait to go in it. I could be such a brat when I wanted to.

It took us a while to get in, without it flipping over on top of us, but once we did, it was amazing: just me and my big sis on the great big sea, the sun beating down on us, and the icing-coloured houses growing smaller and smaller behind us. I looked back at the part of the beach where Mum was sitting with her floppy hat on, but she was just a dot on the horizon, we were so far out. The water was warm and I let my hands glide through it as Ellie rowed and rowed.

'Can you see that?' she exclaimed excitedly, pointing into the water. It was almost clear and you could see right down to the sand and rocks at the bottom. I looked to where she was pointing and saw some starfish, orange and pretty.

'Wow!' I was mesmerized. Everything was beautiful that day. 'Do you think there are mermaids down there, too?'

''Course there are,' said Ellie convincingly. 'You might see one if you stay really still.' I don't know how long we spent totally still, hardly daring to breathe, just staring into the dancing, glittery sea.

'There,' said Ellie suddenly, pointing a little to the left. 'Did you see it?' I followed her finger and stared hard. I thought I saw a flicker of something silvery, but I couldn't be sure. 'There!' she said again, this time more excited. I'd definitely seen it that time, but was it a mermaid? Ellie convinced me it was. They only made themselves known to special people and I was *really* special – or that's what she told me.

'Come on, we'd getter get you back or Mum'll go mad.' Ellie reached back for the oars and started rowing. We'd drifted a bit, but could just make out Mum, now standing and waving to us from the beach.

It was only when we got closer that we noticed she was angry. Apparently we'd been gone over two hours and she'd been going out of her mind, thinking we'd drowned. Ellie took the brunt of Mum's rant. I was just plucked from the dinghy in a huge sandy beach towel and rubbed so dry I turned pink.

Ellie balanced the dinghy on her head as we walked up the beach in our jelly shoes on the way back to the caravan. Even though she was in trouble, she winked at me from underneath it, and I knew neither of us would ever tell our secret. It was ours, just ours.

* * *

I smiled as I lay in bed and remembered that day. It'd been ages since I'd thought about it and it made me feel calmer somehow, almost like she was still with me. It was 5:00am and getting light. I could still hear Mum and Dad talking, interspersed with Dan snoring. There was a soft tap on my door and I whispered, 'Come in.' The door creaked a bit as it opened, and Lee stood there in his pyjamas.

'I can't sleep,' he said blearily. He was rubbing his eyes and looked exhausted.

'Me neither,' I told him. I was still angry about the scene he had caused earlier, but Ellie being missing was hard on all of us and I knew he must have been kept awake with similar thoughts to the ones I was having.

'Were you thinking about her?' I ventured in a hushed voice. He nodded and came and sat on the end of the bed. 'Me too,' I said. 'Do you remember Tenby?' I asked. He smiled and nodded, but it wasn't long before the smile faded away. I didn't know what to say. What could I say? I leaned over and rubbed his arm. 'You okay?' I whispered. He looked at me and took a deep breath. He didn't confirm or deny; he just shrugged.

After a while of sitting in silence, Lee looked at me, biting his lip. 'What?' I asked. I hadn't seen him look so strange. He took another deep breath.

'Do you think she's dead?' he asked, scared of how the question would be received.

'Do you?' I said in a gasp, hardly daring to draw breath. None of us had dared vocalize this before. He shrugged again and I found myself frustrated by such an insubstantial reply. 'Then why did you say it?' I demanded. I was angry he'd put it out there if he wasn't going to do anything about it.

'I don't know. Just forget it.' He pulled himself up from the bed and made to leave.

'Hey,' I said. 'You can't just say that and leave.' I grabbed him by the wrist and pulled him back onto the bed. He didn't put up much of a fight. He obviously needed this as much as I did.

'Well?' I prompted. 'Do you?' After a long, long moment he looked me straight in the eyes.

'I hope to God I'm wrong ...' he began, and my heart sank. I knew he'd lost hope. 'But nothing else makes sense ... does it?'

I started a few sentences, outraged at what he was suggesting, and desperate to prove him wrong. I couldn't finish one of them. I hung my head, the horrible truth knocking me for six. He was right.

NINE

It felt like I'd only been asleep for a few minutes when a distant tapping noise woke me. I lay still and listened out. I didn't even have the energy to open my eyes. Nothing. I must have dreamt it. I rolled over and snuggled back down into my pillows, pulling my duvet over my head and sighing with fatigue. But there it was again. Someone was throwing gravel at my window. I reluctantly hauled myself out of bed to investigate, already pretty sure I knew it'd be Brian. He'd been doing a lot of irrational stuff lately in his attempt to win Zara back.

The weird thing was that I had daydreamed this scenario a hundred times. I longed to have Brian wake me in the night this way to tell me how much he loved me. But it wasn't the middle of the night, and Brian wasn't in love with me. He looked pale and had dark circles under his eyes. He obviously hadn't had much sleep either. He looked pathetic and I felt annoyed, the vision of him and Steph too fresh in my mind.

'Sorry it's so early,' he shouted up at me. 'I really need your help.' I was worried he'd wake Mum and Dad, and the whole street for that matter.

'Shh!' I hissed. 'Stay there; I'll come down.' I closed the

window and pulled on some jeans and a T-shirt, then legged it downstairs to let him in. I was almost sorry I did. He didn't stop talking long enough to draw breath. I was knackered and still a bit preoccupied with thoughts of Ellie. My stomach was gurgling and making me feel sick. I really wasn't in the mood for this.

'She won't take my calls, won't answer my letters, gets her folks to say she's out when I go round there. What else am I meant to do?' he asked, as he paced. Just watching him made me feel dizzy.

'Maybe you should give her some time,' I suggested. I knew from talking to her on the phone that he was driving her mad. He wasn't giving her a chance to sit back and take stock of the situation. He was just in her face the whole time.

'Have you spoken to her?' he asked.

'Yeah,' I replied awkwardly. I saw hope flash in his eyes. 'But not about you,' I added quickly. There was no way I was getting into that whole he-said, she-said thing.

'Do you think there's still a chance?' He suddenly looked fragile and I remembered what I loved about him. I wasn't sure what to say. Zara would rather stick needles in her eyes than get back with him. I didn't want to tell him that. I didn't want to break his heart. I shrugged and he smiled. As long as it wasn't a definitive 'no', then he'd keep trying.

'If you were her, what would you want me to do to prove how much I love you?' he asked, probably thinking we'd have similar tastes, seeing as we were friends. I took some time. He seemed pleased I was giving his dilemma some serious thought.

What was really going on in my head was a whole different story. I really was trying to imagine what he could do to make amends to me if I was his girlfriend. The trouble was, I got stuck on the 'if I was his girlfriend' bit. At one point, I caught myself smiling. I looked up and he was looking at me curiously, those lovely eyes, and those strong hands dwarfing a cup of coffee. I smiled again, heat in my face. He looked encouraged.

'Well?'

'If you want to get her back,' I started, thinking on my feet, 'you should do something totally original. Stupid even. Don't think about how you feel. Just think about how you want her to feel.' He looked blank. 'Public displays of affection always get the girl.'

His eyes widened and his scowl lifted. He jumped to his feet, looking just as wired as when he first arrived. 'You're a genius!' he exclaimed and smacked a kiss on my cheek. 'I know what I'm going to do.'

'What?' I asked, my hand hovering over the place where he'd kissed me. But it was too late; he was gone.

* * *

'Can you come over?' came Zara's voice down the phone a few hours later. She didn't sound happy and I scanned my mind for something, anything, I could have done wrong.

'What's up?' I asked as lightly as I could muster.

'Just get here,' she said and put the phone down. My stomach somersaulted. I wondered if it was something to do with Brian. Maybe she'd found out he was at my house first thing and wasn't happy about it. Maybe Brian had taken my advice and made a big public display, and Zara had hated it and she was going to have a go at me about giving him false hope.

By the time I got to her house I was in a bit of a state.

I'd tried to prepare a few speeches to have at the ready in my defence, but as it turned out, I didn't need them. It sounded like she was having a party. Music was blaring. I knocked on the door for ages and eventually had to call Zara on her mobile to get her to let me in.

I was relieved that she was laughing when she flung the door open. 'Quick!' she giggled, indicating for me to follow her, before legging it upstairs and into her bedroom. I trotted along after her, not having a clue what was going on. In Zara's room, the music was even louder. The windows were open and she was leaning out of one of them. I went to the other, and there in the garden was not just Brian, but the whole band serenading Zara.

The song was pretty dodgy, and out of tune, but it did the business. Zara was melting.

'How romantic is this?' she whispered in my ear, grinning. I smiled. I was glad she was happy, but was just starting to realize I was wholly responsible for sending the guy I adored back into her arms.

'How long have they been here?' I asked. Zara looked at her *Friends* alarm clock and with glee told me it had been almost an hour.

'He says he's not going to stop 'til I've forgiven him.'

'Are you going to?' I was a bit surprised 'cos she'd done nothing but slag him off since the night of the party.

'Eventually,' she said, pleased she was in control.

About ten minutes later she shut the window and we went downstairs. We hid in the kitchen behind the counter. It was my job to carefully peek into the garden and see what they were doing.

Brian had stopped singing and the band had stopped playing. They were just standing around, looking at each other and shrugging, not quite sure what to do. I reported this back to Zara and she smiled before taking a look herself. It was pretty funny and soon our eyes were streaming and we were rolling around the kitchen floor.

Eventually, Zara went out there and put Brian out of his misery. I've never seen anyone so relieved in his life, and I was touched by his capacity to love. We all went back into the house for drinks and snacks, and Brian wouldn't stop going on about how grateful he was for a second chance. Zara knew she had him right where she wanted him and I felt so jealous.

It became pretty obvious that they wanted to be alone, so I helped the others pack up their gear and walked back to town with them. In the cold light of day, Mark wasn't all that. He had horrid blond bum-fluff on his chin and dirty fingernails. When I left them to walk down my road, I felt a bit miserable. Would I ever meet anyone like Brian?

*　*　*

Back at home, it was the calm after the storm. Mum and Dad were in the kitchen preparing a family meal. They thought it was important we were together after all the trauma of the previous day. I wasn't in the mood for it. I felt reflective and tired, and just wanted to be on my own. I went up to my room, intending to have a bit of a nap, but once I lay down, sleep wouldn't come. A few minutes later my mobile rang. It was Brian.

'Thank you so much,' he said, his gratitude making me blush.

'Any time,' I said brightly, trying to make it sound like I meant it.

'No, seriously, I couldn't have done it without you.' I

didn't know what to say to that. I never do when people are praising me.

'I got you something as a thank you,' he said.

'You didn't have to.'

'It's nothing much.'

'Thanks,' I said. 'What is it?'

'Now why would I go and ruin the surprise?' I giggled. 'Listen, we're having band practice at the church hall tomorrow. Why don't you come? Then I can give it to you,' Brian continued.

'Okay.' I was trying desperately not to sound as keen as I felt.

'Cool,' he said. 'See you at five.' The phone clicked and he was gone.

'Oh … my … god,' I thought to myself. Not only did Brian just call me, which was a very rare event, but he also thought I was great and had bought me a present! My mind was racing, wondering what it could be. I wanted to call Zara and tell her, but stopped myself. She was the last person I could tell.

Suddenly, I didn't feel so happy. In fact, I felt quite weepy. I put it down to not having had much sleep, but the world didn't seem so great anymore and I wondered if I'd always be alone.

I sat up on the bed and grabbed my notepad and pen. I began to doodle. The doodles evolved into words, the words into phrases and the phrases (much to my surprise) into a song. I didn't even have to think about it; it was just like I wrote down my thoughts as they came into my head.

I don't know how it had happened. I'd never even written a poem before. But I had a tune and everything for this. I called it Secret Lover, 'cos that's what I was. The minute I allowed the thought into my head, I knew I wouldn't be able to get it out again. This was what I'd been fighting for weeks and weeks. I realized I loved him. Not just fancied, not just a crush, but I loved Brian with every fibre of my being.

TEN

Next morning, Lee got his exam results and they were a disaster. He got a C in Art and the same in English. The rest were mostly Ds and Es. Dad surprised us by being cool about it. It was Mum who flipped out. She couldn't believe any kid of hers could do so badly. She had this really annoying habit of getting stressed about stuff like that after the event. She could've avoided it by being around to make sure he was revising in the first place.

It's not that I begrudged her looking for Ellie. I wish we could all have gone. It's just, well, we needed our mum, too. She was spending all her time and energy on the search, and when she got home, all we got were the grumpy exhausted bits. Sometimes I resented Ellie for taking her away from me, but then I'd get consumed by the most momentous guilt.

Lee did one of his disappearing acts. I think even he was expecting to do a bit better than that and he was embarrassed. He's not great at being the centre of attention when it's family stuff; it freaks him out to have all eyes on him. I ended up feeling sorry for him. It was probably an achievement to pass any exams with all the hassle we'd had in our house that year.

Later on, when he eventually resurfaced, Mum and Dad sat him down for the dreaded talk about his future. They told him they didn't want him to make a decision there and then, but if he wanted, there was always a job for him at the garage.

Then Dan and me got called in. They told us they thought it would be nice if we all went away in the caravan for the weekend. Personally, I could think of nothing worse. I bit my tongue. I didn't want to hurt their feelings by saying I didn't want to go. Dad and Dan were due to take part in a rally somewhere in North Wales and that's where we were going – great.

***

It took me ages to decide what to wear to band practice. I wanted to look nice, but didn't want to make it look obvious I'd made an effort. In the end, I just wore jeans and a vest-top. I spent ages putting make-up on to make it look like I was wearing none at all.

I got there early and was disappointed when for ages it was just me and Mark. It was dead awkward 'cos I think he thought I fancied him. Who could blame him after the way I behaved at the party? I helped him clear some chairs away from the stage and set the microphones up, all the time willing someone else to walk in and save me from the monosyllabic conversation we were trying to force.

The cavalry came in the form of Zara and Abby. I didn't even know Abby was back from Cornwall. The sun had made her freckles come out and she looked dead pretty. A few moments later Brian arrived. My stomach flipped when I saw him and I couldn't help but smile. He smiled back, then went over to Zara and kissed her. It was tough, trying to hide my disappointment.

'You look happy,' said Abby, coming up behind me as I unpacked a carrier bag of snacks and drinks.

'I'm fine,' I lied. 'So tell me more about the surfer bloke you met.' Abby grinned. It had been her favourite and only topic of conversation since she arrived.

'He's gorgeous,' she swooned, helping herself to a choc-ice. 'He's really brown and muscly, and has amazing blue eyes.' I kept a smile plastered on my face, but my mind and eyes were wandering. Brian looked so intense as he started to sing. He closed his eyes and looked as though he was really feeling the music.

'Are you listening?' Abby's shrill voice sounded annoyed. It made me jump, and the boys, too. Brian stopped singing and looked over at us, irritated we had disturbed his rhythm.

'Sorry,' I mumbled, not sure which of them to direct it to. Abby looked over to see what could have possibly taken my attention from hearing about the surfer. My heart missed a beat as her eyes rested on Brian for a second. Thankfully, she didn't even entertain the thought and moved her inquisitive stare to Mark. Her eyes stopped there and an evil smile crept in from the corner of her mouth.

'You fancy him, don't you?' she demanded, nodding at Mark.

'No!' I said. But it was too late. She was already enjoying this too much.

'Oi, Zar.' Zara looked up from her magazine. 'Looks like Lisa needs a bit of help getting it on with Mark.'

'As if!' I was aware that Brian was listening to the conversation. If Brian could hear from up there on the stage, then Mark probably could too, and I really didn't want to do anything to encourage him. Zara shut her magazine and came over.

'I thought you liked him.'

'I don't.'

'I saw you looking!' said Abby, incredulous that I was trying to deny it.

'It'd be great if you two started going out. We could go on double dates and everything,' enthused Zara. I said nothing. It was easier to go along with the lie. 'Come on, let's go and talk to him,' she said. They grabbed an arm each and dragged me over.

Brian came towards us to grab some refreshments for himself and the rest of the band. He looked intrigued and was smiling.

'What are you doing?' he asked Zara.

'Out of the way!' she exclaimed, jokily pushing past him. 'This is an emergency and Dr Love is on call.' Brian didn't look any the wiser and I was dying of embarrassment. 'Lisa fancies Mark and you told me he fancied her ...' This was news to me. Had Brian and Zara been talking about me?

'Well, he said she was pretty good at the bass,' he explained, a look of pity on his face. He knew I wasn't enjoying this.

'Same thing,' said Zara, pushing me up on the stage. Mark looked just as mortified as I was. I tried to wriggle out of it, but Abby and Zara are pretty strong when they have you in their grip. Luckily for me, Mark smiled awkwardly and headed for the loo. Abby and Zara probably would have dragged me in there too if I hadn't escaped outside.

* * *

I was sitting on a concrete step, writing my name in the

dry mud with a twig, when Brian came outside and sat next to me.

'So …' he said, '… you and Mark, hey?' He grinned at me.

'It's not like that.'

'He's cool,' he said. 'He'll look after you,' he continued. I didn't look up from the twig. I didn't say anything. There was nothing to say. This whole thing was getting way out of hand. 'Want me to ask him out for you?'

'No!' I snapped and immediately regretted it. Brian pulled a face at me. He wasn't quite sure what he'd done wrong. 'I don't even like him like that. Zara and Abby are just having a laugh,' I explained, trying to make my voice sound calmer so as not to freak him out. 'Oh,' he said, looking more than a little confused.

We sat there like that for a while, me playing with the dirt, him watching me, neither of us speaking. I didn't want to talk to him, didn't know what to say; but I wanted him there. It felt nice having him next to me, feeling his knee touching mine.

He stood up and I looked at him. I didn't want him to go. He put his hand in his pocket and must have noticed the look of alarm on my face, as he sat back down again.

'I forgot about your present,' he said, smiling again and handing me a small paper bag. I felt terrible for snapping at him as I took it.

'Thanks,' I mumbled. I opened it up and inside was a leather friendship bracelet. It wasn't my usual style, but I liked it 'cos he gave it to me.

'Do you like it?' he asked. I was lost for words and just nodded. ''Cos you can change it if you don't.'

'It's lovely,' I said, stroking it.

'Here,' he said, taking it out of my hands, 'I'll put it on

for you.' I reached out my arm and rested it on his leg as he wrestled for a while with the stiff popper. It was a bit big, but there was no way I was going to let it fall off. There was no way I was even going to take it off, ever. 'It looks great,' he said, pleased with his choice.

'Thanks,' I said, looking up at him. I held his eyes for a little too long. I didn't want to break the moment; this was just me and him, and I wanted to enjoy it while it lasted. Suddenly, I felt really brave and leaned over and kissed him on the cheek. 'That was really thoughtful.' He smiled back at me and I thought I was going to melt.

'This looks cosy.' We turned round to see Abby leaning on the door jamb, arms crossed over her chest.

'Look what Brian gave me,' I said, perhaps a bit too gushily, as I showed her my new bracelet.

'It's for her help getting me and Zara back together,' butted in Brian. He looked a bit nervous.

'If you say so,' she replied, seeming a little bored. 'They're ready to get back to it, if you can break away from your tête-à-tête, Bri,' she said sarcastically. Brian and I both stood up. He brushed himself down and headed back inside. Abby didn't do much to move out of his way as he squeezed past.

Then there was just me and Abby. I was trying not to grin too madly, but I felt so happy.

'Don't even go there,' Abby hissed in my ear as I too pushed my way past her.

'What are you talking about?' I said, my heart beating way too fast and my legs turning to jelly.

'You know what I mean,' she warned, before heading back over to Zara, leaving me by the door feeling like a nervous wreck.

ELEVEN

I really didn't want to go to Wales in the caravan. It was the last weekend before school started again and Zara was having a sleepover, which I really didn't want to miss. I was worried Abby had worked out I had a thing for Brian, and without me there to stop her there was a real and present danger she'd blab to Zara.

We set off far too early for my liking. Lee got to go in the rally car with Dan and listen to great music and generally look cool. I had to endure Mum and Dad rowing about directions and listening to some rubbish comedian on an audio book. I wondered how on earth I was going to make it through a dull weekend talking about cars with my dull family.

When we were kids, the caravan seemed huge and there were loads of places to hide. When I was fifteen, it suddenly felt tiny, and there was absolutely nowhere to hide. I had a bit of a moan about it to Lee. He didn't see my problem. Bear in mind that this is the brother who used the excuse-for-a-toilet while we were all in earshot. Mum stood up for me when Dad got a bit grumpy about my complaining, and said I could sleep in the tent attachment with Dan and Lee. The thought of this was gross enough in itself, but it wasn't half as gross as having to listen to Mum and Dad toss and turn all night.

Dad, Dan and Lee went straight down to the track to register for the race. I got roped in to helping Mum make sandwiches for lunch. Why do parents always choose times like that to have a right-on chat? Mum was really fishing for me to tell her if I had anyone 'special' in my life at the moment – as if I could tell her anything about Brian. She didn't take the hint that my silence meant I didn't want to talk about it, and then launched into a great big nostalgia-fest about when she first started going out with Dad – yeuch.

Dad got in even more of a strop with me when I told him I didn't really want to go down to the track. What was I going to do there? It was just a heaving, smelly pit of testosterone and I could think of nothing more boring. He threw the old 'this is meant to be a family weekend' card at me, and just to shut him up, I agreed I'd go and watch the actual race if I could go to the shops for a bit first. I thought Mum might be up for it too, but she seemed tense and stuck to Dad like glue, probably to monitor how much he was drinking.

Finally, the boys got their overalls on and hauled all their tools down to the track, Mum following with her fold-up chair and some magazines. I felt a bit sentimental when she put her floppy hat on. It reminded me of when we were young, when we were *all* in the caravan, when we were happy.

* * *

The town turned out to be a bit of a hole. There was about one decent shop, a dodgy-looking pub and a Spar on the corner. I got bored quickly and was trying to think of something I could do, when I saw a bus stop over the road saying we were only a few miles from a much bigger place. I checked the times and there was a bus due in just a few minutes. There were loads coming back every hour too. I could easily make it back in time for the race at three.

Luckily, there weren't too many people on the bus. It was so hot; the driver said the air conditioning had broken, and the tiny open windows weren't providing much relief. I didn't mind really. It was nice just to be on my own after feeling like a sardine all day. I rested my forehead on the window and looked at the fields and trees as they whizzed past in a bit of a blur.

I got off and felt spoilt for choice. I didn't have much cash, but I decided I'd get Dad and Dan a good luck present for the race, to show them my support. First, I went to Starbucks and treated myself to a huge caramel frappuccino and a cheese twist. I couldn't really stomach the sandwiches in the caravan, as the air was still a bit ripe after Lee's visit to the toilet.

I didn't really know what I was looking for as a present, but knew I'd know it when I saw it. I was in one of those moods when I could have happily ambled about all day. I turned up a side street and saw a really old-fashioned jeweller's. In the window they had some pewter tankards. I remembered Dad used to have one that his parents had bought him for his twenty-first, but it had got lost in the move and he'd been gutted.

I counted my money. I didn't have enough to buy one each, but they could share it. After all, they were a partnership in this race. I smiled when I imagined them sitting on the bonnet in their orange overalls and drinking their winners' champagne from it. I went inside and a bell rang above the door, making me jump. A little old man with half-moon specs came and served me. He said he could engrave it if I wanted to wait.

I sat on a threadbare chair in the corner. I think it used to be red velvet at one stage. As I was drumming my fingers, I caught a glimpse of my friendship bracelet from Brian. I pulled my sleeve up and admired it. It really was beautiful and so was he. I felt a flush of guilt, knowing, as always, that I had to be on guard. This was my secret. Then I remembered I was so far away from Abby and Zara and Hollyoaks that there was no way they could know what I was thinking, and I indulged myself in a little daydream about Brian and me on a beach at sunset.

* * *

It was later than I expected when I came out of the shop with my package. The bus seemed to stop all round the world on the way back, so I had to hurry down to the track. I looked for ages, but couldn't see any of my family. It was pretty crowded, though.

I got the lady at the information desk to make an announcement for Mum to come and get me. I waited for almost half an hour, but she didn't turn up. I thought they must be back at the caravan, though I couldn't really think of a reason why. Maybe the car had broken down or something? I headed back there myself.

As soon as I passed the shower blocks and turned the corner into our row, I knew something was up. Mum, Dan and Lee were all sitting at the picnic table, looking miserable. Dad was pacing nearby, looking red and angry. Mum jumped up when she saw me and came running over with open arms.

'There she is!' she exclaimed, grabbing me and hugging me as if she hadn't seen me just a few hours before.

'What's up?' I asked, looking at each of them in turn.

'We've probably missed the race, thanks to you.' Dan glared at me. I was shocked. What had I done? The afternoon had been so nice; the last thing I was expecting was to come back to a scene like this.

'What have I done?' Hot tears were threatening. I was outraged at the injustice of it all.

'You said you'd be an hour,' said Dad. I still didn't see why everyone was so wound up. 'That was nearly three hours ago.'

'Sorry,' I said, still a little dumbfounded. I remembered the present and thought it might soften his mood if I were to give it to him now. 'I got you this,' I said, offering it to him. 'I was so long because I had to wait to get it engraved.' I was still holding it out in my hands, but Dad didn't take it. I tried to offer it to Dan, but Dad knocked it out of my hands.

'We don't want your stupid tat,' he yelled. 'That's not going to help us win the race, is it?' I couldn't believe he was being so cruel. 'We have just wasted valuable time looking for you when we should have been fine-tuning the car. How about you try being a bit less selfish for the rest of the weekend?' With that, he walked off, Lee and Dan behind him. I felt like I'd been punched in the guts.

'Why is it such a big deal?' I wailed at Mum as she started putting stuff in the van, ready to head back down to the track herself.

'Come on, Lisa, think. Every day he has to face the fact that one of his daughters is missing.'

'We all do,' I mumbled angrily under my breath.

'I know,' she said, a little more kindly. 'But you know what he's like. Why do you have to wind him up all the time?' I shrugged. 'Come on. Let's just forget about it and try and have a nice weekend. Are you coming?'

'No!' I said, still outraged. 'I just spent all my money on a good luck present for them, and look at it,' I yelled, nodding at the package lying under the table, where Dad had knocked it. 'Why should I come and watch their stupid race after they treated me like that?' Mum sighed. She didn't want to get into this.

'Suit yourself,' she said, grabbing her floppy hat and heading off.

* * *

I was furious by that stage. It's one thing to be treated so unfairly, but quite another to have your audience walk away from you when you're trying to have a rant. I slammed back into the caravan and threw myself onto Mum and Dad's already made-up bed. I imagined Zara and Abby having great fun without me. I bet they hadn't even noticed I wasn't there.

A little while later, I got up and looked in the cool-box. I fancied some chocolate, but there wasn't any, just a few cans of Lilt. I didn't really want one, but I took one anyway and sat at the table, looking out of the window. The plastic was a bit scratched, but I could still see a dad trying to have a game of cricket with his toddlers while a mum sunbathed with her book. My lip curled as I watched them. How come they were so happy?

By the time I finished my drink, it was warm and flat, but I was still angry. Mum had left one of her quiz books open with a pen resting in the spine. I tried to do one, but got bored when I got stuck. I pushed the tip of the biro into the can and it made a perfect hole. The plastic scraped against the metal as I pulled it out. I did it again and then again, all the way round until I had cut the can in two. I put the two pieces rough side up on the table, then leaned my head sideways on my forearm as I contemplated them. They looked so inviting.

Without even thinking about what I was doing, I lifted my arm above them and cautiously brought it down. The sharp edges tickled at first, I was touching them so lightly. I pressed harder, intrigued to see how much I could endure. I was enjoying this.

After holding my arm down for a whole minute, I lifted it and looked at all the dents and impressions left behind. I tried to do the same with my left arm, but I was clumsy and slipped, breaking the skin. At first I panicked. I was in shock and worried at the sight of blood. I expected the pain to rush in at any moment, but it didn't. It was almost the reverse, like all the anger and annoyance I had felt towards my family rushed out.

I watched it for ages, entranced by the pattern as it darkened and eventually turned hard. I gently rubbed my fingers over it. It was like a kind of Braille, a secret code that only I understood.

TWELVE

Dad and Dan got disqualified from the race for starting late. Of course, they blamed me, and the rest of the weekend was pure hell. I couldn't stand the thought of being stuck in the car with Mum and Dad again on the way home, not with Dad barely speaking to me. I went in Dan's car with him and Lee instead. His driving always makes me want to puke, but it was better than the alternative.

It was when we stopped off for petrol and sweets that Lee announced he didn't fancy getting a job just yet and maybe he'd go back to school. I tried to talk him out of it. The last thing I wanted was him cramping my style in my exam year. My protests only made him more certain. He reckoned he was too young to start paying Mum and Dad rent, and year 11 must be a doss the second time around, or that's what his mate Bombhead had told him – he was re-taking, too.

I tried to call Zara when I got back, but her sister said she wasn't in. She didn't know where she was or what time she'd be back, only that she'd gone off somewhere with Abby. I felt uneasy, like the weekend away with my family had somehow weakened my position in the group. I tried not to think about it as I laid my uniform out that night and packed up my school bag. Things had to be good that year. If I did well and passed my exams, it could be my ticket out of there.

I didn't sleep well that night. I never do the night before a new term. I couldn't eat much breakfast 'cos I felt nervous. I didn't even know why. I made sure I didn't walk to school with Lee and I totally ignored him once we were there. I'd have been happy to pretend I'd never met him before in my life.

I made my way to my new form room and was glad Steph was already there. She seemed just as relieved to see me, knowing Zara still hadn't forgiven her for sleeping with Brian. I sat next to her and we chatted, but I kept looking at the door, waiting for Zara and Abby to arrive, wondering how they would be with me.

'Good summer?' she asked. She was far more relaxed than I was.

'It was all right.' I wrinkled my nose. 'Nothing to write home about.'

'Mine neither,' she said, then realized I wasn't really interested. 'What's up with you?' she probed. 'You're not in a strop with me about Brian as well, are you?'

'No,' I assured her, 'I just get a bit edgy on the first day back.'

'Sad cow,' she muttered. Didn't I know it?

Zara made a big deal of walking in arm-in-arm with Brian. When she saw Steph, she shot her daggers. Steph just raised her eyes and shook her head. 'Get over it, Zara. You're not in any danger. It was a hideous drunken mistake, one I thankfully can't remember that much about.' Brian looked nervous. You could see he just wanted the ground to open up and swallow him whole.

Zara tutted loudly and went and sat on the other side of the room, behind Brian and Noel, bagsying the seat next to her for Abby. I tried to catch her eye, but she wouldn't look at me. I felt panicky inside when I realized how stupid I was to sit next to Steph. Zara must have thought I was on her side, which I wasn't. I didn't want to be on anyone's side; I just wanted us all to get on.

I knew if I moved seats now, it would offend Steph, and she was a nightmare when she was in a strop with you. At the same time, Zara had the potential to be worse. At that moment Abby arrived. She made a big thing of ignoring Steph, and me as well by association. She walked over to sit by Zara, who was grinning back her approval of the silent treatment.

I bit the bullet and pushed my chair back, thinking I should at least say hello. I made my way over and perched on a nearby empty desk.

'Hiya,' I said, as brightly as I could, but neither of them looked up. It was Brian who turned around and said hello first, and suddenly I didn't feel so nervous.

'We've got band practice later if you fancy it?'

'Thanks, that would be great,' I said, returning his smile.

Zara caught his eye and glared at him. He looked unsure what he had done wrong, so turned back and talked with the other lads again. Zara looked at me as if she'd only just noticed I was there.

'Oh hi,' she said, easily, with a big grin on her face. 'How was the drag racing weekend?' She and Abby both sniggered.

'Rallying,' I corrected.

'Whatever,' she added coolly.

'It was pants,' I said, 'as per usual.' Neither of them seemed that interested and looked as though they were going to turn away from me again to continue their conversation. 'So how was the sleepover?' I asked, determined that they weren't going to blank me. Zara looked at Abby, then at me.

'Very interesting,' she said, looking right into the core of me. I felt my entire body turn to ice.

* * *

Lunchtime couldn't come fast enough. Morning lessons seemed to drag on and on, with all the teachers giving us the same old speech about how important our GCSE year was. At least it gave me time to think about what I should do about Zara and Abby. I wasn't really sure if they were just being funny with me, or they were just acting tough with everyone. I'd watched them trying to intimidate some new kids in year seven at first break.

I went and sat with them at lunchtime. I figured if I just acted normally, then they would have to do the same. They didn't ignore me, which was something, but they only spoke to me when I asked them questions. I was starting to get annoyed about it. What exactly had I done wrong?

Just when I was psyching myself up to confront them, Lee and Bombhead came over and there was no way I could pretend I didn't know them.

'Alright, sis?' Lee squeezed onto the bench next to me. Bombhead sat opposite. Out of the corner of my eye, I could see Abby and Zara looking interested.

'What do you want?' I hissed. He'd promised me he wouldn't do this.

'Don't be like that,' he teased. 'Aren't you going to

Why would anyone want to make friends with a freak like me?

It's weird to think that once upon a time I loved swimming.

The one thing Zara was good at was making me feel bad, and now she had a good reason.

I didn't have a clue what was happening in my own head, let alone Mum's.

I knew the whole world
would find out if Lee didn't
keep his mouth shut.

I could take anything they said about me, as long as I had Brian.

If I did it, I knew I'd feel all right for ten minutes tops, and then I'd hate myself.

Dad said that until I stopped
cutting myself, I didn't have
a right to privacy.

I hated him and loved
him and missed him
all at the same time.

All the card said was 'Happy Christmas, love E.' Didn't she have anything else to say to us?

I tried to imagine life without
cutting. It terrified me, but deep
down I knew I was strong enough.

introduce us?' He looked hopefully at Abby and nicked a chip off my plate.

'Zara, Abby, this is my brother, Lee,' I said, under duress. Bombhead cleared his throat very unsubtly. 'And this is Bombhead.' Zara and Abby ignored Bombhead. Who wouldn't? He's a scruffy, stinky freak. They did, however, go all girly and giggly with Lee. This was all I needed – my two supposed best friends getting on better with my brother than they did with me.

'Did you want something?' I demanded, when I thought they were making themselves a little too comfortable.

'You couldn't lend us some money, could you?' Lee had his puppy-dog eyes on. He was good at those.

'No, I couldn't.' Never lend Lee money unless you don't want to see it again. Abby reached into her purse and pulled out a quid.

'This any good?' He held her eyes as he reached out and took it.

'Pay you back tomorrow?' he offered.

'Any time,' she purred. Yeuck, I thought to myself. This really was too much.

When Lee and Bombhead had gone, Abby and Zara were much more friendly. They wanted to know all about him and why I hadn't told them sooner that he'd be doing re-takes. I felt like reminding them that they had been giving me the cold shoulder until a few minutes ago, but I didn't. I let it drop, as I always did.

**

We had double Maths straight after lunch, followed by double P.E. – what an afternoon! I was dawdling on my way to P.E. I didn't want to go 'cos it was swimming. All the boys were heading out to the playing field for cross-country running. I passed Brian on his way. He looked as though he was looking forward to it as much as I was.

I smiled at him and walked past. I didn't really have much to say to him and I didn't want Zara and Abby to see me talking to him. It would have only fuelled the fire of their suspicion.

'Hey,' he said a moment after passing me.

'Hey yourself,' I replied, aware that it sounded a bit cheesy.

'Can you sing?' I looked at him blankly. What kind of question was that on a Tuesday afternoon?

'I suppose,' I said, my face wrinkled with confusion. 'Why?'

'We want a female vocalist for the band. Might balance the sound out a bit – would you be interested?'

'Yeah,' I said, sounding a bit too eager. 'I'll have a go,' I added, trying to dilute it a little.

'Cool. I'll let you know when and where.'

I had a hop, skip and a jump about me as I headed over to the pool. Maybe things weren't so bad after all.

Everyone else was changed by the time I got there. Steph noticed me smiling and wanted to know what it was all about. 'Nothing,' I sang, but she still looked suspicious.

'Who is he?' she demanded, grinning.

'Who is what?' said Zara, she and Abby coming out of the same cubicle.

'No one,' I said firmly, giving Steph a look of warning to drop it.

I used to love swimming. I got all my badges before I was twelve. But things change when you get older. I felt awkward about my body anyway, but especially so 'cos of the cuts on my arms from the Lilt can. I'd covered them up with plasters and kept my T-shirt on, so that no one would see. They'd only ask questions, and then what would I say?

Luckily, a few girls in my class wore T-shirts over their costumes, so I didn't look too out of place. It wasn't such a bad lesson, really. I liked floating around thinking of Brian. The possibility of singing in the band with him and spending all that time with him made me want to squeal.

'Ow!' Steph had thrown a float at my head.

'Pay attention,' she chided, pretending to be Mrs Mitchell. I stuck my tongue out, making the real Mrs Mitchell blow her whistle at me. I could see Zara and Abby laughing.

Just before the end of the lesson, we all had to get out and either jump or dive off the board. I was glad I was in my T-shirt. It's horrible being all cold and soggy in front of everyone else. As we were queuing up, Zara and Abby pushed in so they were next to me.

'Eurgh, she's peeling!' screeched Abby, pointing at my arm. I looked down and was horrified to see one of my plasters hanging off. I covered it up quickly as the line shuffled along a bit.

'So,' said Zara, meaning business. 'Are you going to tell us who this mystery bloke you fancy is?'

'I don't fancy any bloke,' I shrugged, hoping they'd buy it.

'What, are you some kind of lesbian?' said Abby, making sure everyone could hear.

'Ha ha.' I wasn't in the mood for this.

'If you don't tell us,' said Zara with an evil grin in her eye, 'we'll chuck you in.' She and Abby each grabbed hold of one of my arms.

'You wouldn't,' I challenged, giggling with nerves.

SPLASH!

Oh yes they would. It felt like I was under water for ages, getting tossed around in a huge washing machine. The water rushed up my nose and down my throat, and started stinging my eyes. My arms and legs were flailing as I tried to stop my body spinning. If only I could get my head facing up, I knew I could get to the surface in time. The surface of the water was coming down on me too slowly. There was a weird warped silence and I thought I was going to suffocate.

Just in time, I broke the skin of the water, coughing and spluttering and gasping for air. My wet hair had formed a shell around my ear and all I could hear was a sound like the wailing of an arctic wind. My eyes were blurry, but I could see them pointing and laughing, and when the water finally emptied from my ears, I could hear Zara shrieking with laughter.

'Eurgh, look at that string of snot coming from her nose!' I wiped it away but it was too late; they'd all seen and were laughing at me. I wished I could go back under the water and stay there forever, like the mermaids Ellie had told me about.

THIRTEEN

I got used to being the butt of their jokes soon enough. They said it was 'cos they knew I could take it and made it sound like a sign of affection. Stupidly, I believed them. I thought the only way they'd let me be friends with them was if I entertained them. I tried my hardest to fit the role, but it wasn't me; I was a clumsy clown.

As the day for the band audition drew closer, I wondered if I even wanted to go for it. The thought of standing up there on a stage and singing in front of everyone made me feel sick. What if I made a total fool of myself in front of Brian? What if I tried to sing and nothing came out but a squeak or a grumble? I'd die. I knew it was getting to me, as I was starting to have nightmares about it. I decided I wasn't going to put myself through it, and told Abby and Zara that I wasn't going to bother.

'Come on, don't be such a spoil-sport,' said Abby. She seemed surprised I wasn't as into the idea of becoming a rock star as she was.

'It'll be a laugh. We're all going to have a go,' said Zara. This was news to me and a huge blow. I thought Brian had only asked me. I'd been basking in that glory for days. If it wasn't for Zara and Abby's powers of persuasion, I'd have backed out there and then.

I still had very cold feet about the whole thing when we turned up at the hall at lunchtime. They were rigging up lights and microphones, and everything. This wasn't going to be a small deal. I decided I wouldn't go through with it. I'd catch Brian on his own and have a word, then slip off home without anyone noticing – or that was my plan at least.

I should have known that Zara would be on my case if I went within a metre of him. I cornered him backstage and tried to explain about my change of heart.

'It's not that I don't like your music,' I told him. The truth was I loved it, but then I loved everything about him. 'And I like hanging out with you guys,' I added, when he didn't fill the silence I'd left for him. 'It's just, you know, it's a big year with exams and everything. I just don't think I should take on another commitment.'

'The rest of us manage okay,' he said, not unkindly. 'Sometimes it's good to take your mind off school work and really go wild.'

'I just don't think it's for me,' I said weakly. 'Some people are just meant to be on stage,' I said, looking at Zara and Abby messing about with the microphones. '… And some should stay out of sight and not embarrass themselves.' Brian looked saddened by this, as if I'd really let him down. I felt like a cow.

'At least have a go. We've got everything set up now.' I'd become convinced that he'd just asked me 'cos I was there and it was polite. But maybe, just maybe, he really wanted me in the band. I felt a warm feeling spread through my chest.

'Okay.' What harm could it do? He grinned at me and rushed off to help Noel bring the drums in. As I turned round, there they were, Zara and Abby, leaning on the wall at the back of the stage, looking me up and down. I quickly dropped my smile and tried to act casual with them, but they weren't having any of it and I suddenly felt tense.

***

Luckily, I didn't pull the short straw and have to go first. Abby did. She loved being up there with everyone looking at her, especially when Lee and Bombhead sneaked in. She did some really sexy moves and looked straight at Lee. God knows why – he's gross. I thought she was pretty good, but the band didn't seem to think so. They asked her to stop after two verses. She shrugged as she left the stage. She didn't really want to be in the band anyway and was quite pleased at the chance to go and flirt with Lee at the back of the hall.

Zara went next and she was bad. I mean, there are people who need a bit of tuning and then there are people who are tone deaf. It was quite embarrassing listening to her. Unlike Abby, she was taking herself seriously and really giving it some. Brian looked horrified that this ghastly noise could come out of his girlfriend's mouth. I caught his eye and it made me giggle. Unfortunately for me, Zara saw me. She stopped dead and bellowed into the microphone.

'You think you can do any better?' I felt like everyone was looking at me. It certainly wiped the smile off my face. Brian went over to her and tried to calm her down, but you can't when she's off on one. I gulped hard. She stomped down the stage steps and came over to me. 'Go on then. Let's see what you're made of,' she hissed before heading over to Abby and co.

I took a deep breath and got to my feet. By this time, even people who weren't trying out had milled in, 'cos it had started raining outside. My heart was thumping as I walked onto the stage. Although Brian had lent me a tape, I didn't really know the song that well. Noel cued me in on the drums, but it didn't feel right, probably 'cos Zara was glaring at me, arms crossed.

'Sorry,' I mumbled. 'Can we try again?'

'Yeah, 'cos we've got all day,' shouted Lee from the back of the hall. I could have killed him. I closed my eyes and steadied my breathing. I could do this. All I had to do was stay calm. Noel cued me in again and I heard the guitars start up. I closed my eyes and leaned into the microphone. I hadn't even sung a whole word when there was an awful screech. Everyone had to put their fingers in their ears. Zara looked satisfied. She'd messed with the volume and now everyone was laughing at me, again.

I wanted to just cut my losses and go. I was only doing this as a favour to Brian and even he looked as though he was losing patience.

'Just breathe easy and take it slow,' he advised, as he adjusted the volume and made sure I was looking him right in the eye and not focusing on anything else. I did as I was told. The music started and I sang. It wasn't great, but it wasn't bad. I lasted about a verse before Zara made it impossible for me to continue. I'd done my bit for Brian. I wasn't going to stay and be humiliated. I left the stage and walked out of the hall.

'Where are you going?' demanded Abby, still laughing with Zara at the most recent joke at my expense.

'Geography,' I replied coolly. None of them tried to stop me. They didn't even want me to stay. I couldn't believe Lee was being so chummy with them and joining in with them being so immature, but then I remembered: that is his speciality.

'Is she always this boring?' I heard Zara ask as I left. I was sure she'd intended for me to hear.

'She's much worse at home,' came his reply. He was obviously trying to impress them.

* * *

I felt quite miserable when I got home. Zara and Abby had teased me all afternoon about not being able to take a joke. I was lying on my bed listening to some music and trying to do my History homework. I really couldn't get my head around all that Second World War stuff.

Respite came in the form of a text message. My stomach flipped when I saw it was from Brian. All it said was: 'You're in!' I couldn't believe it. Did they really want me for the band? I called him straightaway. He couldn't just send me two words when I suddenly had a million questions.

'It's me!' I said as soon as he answered.

'Hello me,' he said. I could tell he was smiling. I wondered if he thought I might be Zara from the warmth in his voice.

'It's Lisa.'

'I know.'

'So you got my message then?'

'Yeah!' I gushed, feeling a bit breathless. 'Does this mean what I think it means?'

'Yeah.' He seemed amused by my excitement.

'Really?' I asked, unable to believe it.

'It was unanimous. You were the best by far.'

'Zara's not going to be too happy about it.'

'You leave her to me. You just make sure you're at practice tomorrow. We've got a gig next week and you need to learn all the songs. But don't worry, I'll help you.' It was all getting a bit too much for me to take in. A gig already?

'I'll be there,' I said, and wished I hadn't. I never managed to sound cool when I was talking to him.

'Wicked,' he said. 'See you in the morning then.'

'Yeah, see you.' I held the phone to my ear for a few more moments, draining the last echoes of his voice from it.

Mum called us for tea and I bounded downstairs three at a time.

'You're a psycho, you are,' said Lee. 'You were miserable half an hour ago.'

'And now I'm not,' I trilled.

'Any particular reason?' asked Dad from behind his paper.

'I just got picked to sing vocals in Brian's band,' I said, hardly able to contain my excitement. That'll show him, I thought. It'd prove I wasn't a total waste of space.

'That's wonderful, love,' said Mum as she put the casserole on the table. Lee turned his nose up at it.

'She's not doing it.' My heart sank. Surely Dad wasn't going to mess this up for me, too?

FOURTEEN

Mum came into my room later that night for a 'chat'. I really wasn't in the mood for it, thinking it would be an update on the search for Ellie. Surprisingly, it was about me. Even more surprisingly, it was about me and the band. She said I should keep going with it, but keep it under my hat. She said she'd speak to Dad when he was in a better mood. She was in for a long, long wait.

Once Zara had stopped giving me a hard time for making it into the band, I really started to enjoy myself. It was fun learning all the songs and experimenting with my voice. I also liked the fact that I was getting to spend a lot more time with Brian, even if we weren't exactly alone – Zara made sure of that.

To keep her sweet about not making it into the band herself, Brian had made her image consultant for all of us, whatever that was meant to be. So every rehearsal, there she was with Abby, tearing out pictures from maga-zines of things she liked the look of. It was a fruitless task really, 'cos none of us had any spare cash to spend on clothes, but hey, it kept her happy.

I dreaded what she was going to put me in for the gig. Knowing her and her warped sense of humour, it would be hideous. I was actually pleasantly surprised. She and Abby had pooled together some of their clothes to come up with a really funky outfit. I couldn't wait to get it home and try it on.

I skipped dinner and went straight to my room. It was all pretty tight-fitting, but I felt good in it, really sexy. I was trying out some different styles with my make-up and admiring myself in the mirror when Dad walked in without knocking. I hate it when he does that.

'What *are* you wearing?' The tone of his voice told me he disapproved. He didn't really need to pull the face as well.

'Don't you ever knock?' I replied, hoping I'd managed to avoid the question. He handed the portable to me.

'Phone for you. And don't stay on too long. We're not made of money.' I raised my eyes to heaven as I shut the door behind him. How many times had I heard that?

'How does it look?' It was Zara.

'Great,' I replied. 'Thanks.'

'No problem,' she said. We chatted for a while, and when I hung up I was glad that things seemed to be back to normal between us.

***

I was dead nervous when the day of the gig came. It was a pretty big deal for all of us, but especially for me as I'd had to lie to my parents about where I was going. Mum had tried to talk to Dad for me and he was absolutely adamant I couldn't be in the band. He didn't like the look of Brian or his mates and thought they were trouble.

There was no way I was going to back out, so I told them I was going to stay at Zara's for the night to work on some Geography coursework. So I sneaked out of the house with my costume in my bag and got there just in the nick of time.

The first half went well, and I was surprised by how comfortable I felt performing to a huge crowd. Zara and Abby said we sounded great, but I think they were both a bit drunk – they'd been getting some of the older lads to buy them drinks from the bar.

It was all going pretty well and we'd just started on our last song when I looked into the crowd and froze to the spot. Oh … my … God. Standing there, glaring at me with a face of thunder, was Dad. I tried to carry on with the song, but I totally lost the rhythm and the words fled from my mind. It was like a nightmare. I was standing on a stage with loads of people staring at me and I couldn't speak, let alone sing, my throat was stone dry.

Luckily Brian realized something was up and pretended there was a technical fault with the speakers. He called a break. Dad started coming towards me. I knew he was going to make a scene. I wanted to run, but I couldn't move and then he was shouting at me, in front of everyone as he always does.

He bellowed at me. 'Don't you think having one daughter go missing on me is bad enough?' I couldn't believe he'd brought Ellie up in front of all those people. No one knew. As a family, we'd decided that's how we were going to keep it, just between us.

He must have been drinking. 'Every day your mother and I face the fact that Ellie could be dead. Have you any idea what I was going through not knowing where you were?' I could see Abby and Zara looking on in interest. It was almost like they had ringside seats. I wasn't going to let him humiliate me in front of my mates again, so I legged it.

I ran home and locked myself in the bathroom. I didn't know what to do. Mum was at work at the chemist's so she couldn't even protect me. I felt jittery and sick. I knew I was in for the hiding of my life. I needed something to calm me down and reached for the only thing I could think of.

There was something quite ironic about using Dad's razor to cut myself. I didn't do it too deeply and it didn't even hurt, but it did do the trick. Just seeing the red come out of me brought everything back into focus. I felt lucid again, and suddenly I knew exactly what I should do. I carefully cleaned my new cut, then dabbed it in cream and wrapped it in loads of toilet roll. Then I ran to my room, grabbed my rucksack and started packing.

I was looking for my building society book when I heard the front door slam. My blood ran cold and I hoped it would be either Lee or Dan. The heavy, unsteady footsteps coming up the stairs told me it was. I hid the bag under my bed and braced myself. I could stand him yelling at me for as long as it took, 'cos I knew I was out of there.

***

Dad didn't yell at me for that long, really. I decided my best tactic would be to not answer back and just take it. I knew if I didn't put up a fight he'd soon get bored and leave me alone. I think he must have been drinking loads, 'cos he was kind of swaying as he yelled at me and he kept losing the thread of what he was saying, then repeating himself, over and over.

I think he must have gone back to the pub, 'cos when I sneaked downstairs the drinks cabinet was ransacked and the fridge door was hanging open. For once I was grateful that there was no beer in the house. I didn't leave a note as my arm was just getting sore and I was worried I'd bleed on the paper.

I felt frightened, sneaking out into the night, but it was exciting, too. I wondered if this was how Ellie had felt. I stuck to the places I knew and thought about trying to sneak into school. I knew I'd be safe there, but then I remembered about the ghost in the locker room and I got the spooks. Who was I trying to kid? There was no way I could spend a night in that place on my own.

I went back to The Loft, where we'd been playing the gig, but the bouncer wouldn't believe I just wanted to go in to have a look for my friends. I decided I'd go round the back and wait for the others there, but the van had gone and that meant so had my friends. I started walking to Zara's house, but when I got there all the lights were out. I didn't want to wake the whole family up, 'cos if I did, her parents would only make me go home.

I remembered that Brian and the rest of the band stored their equipment in a church hall near his house. Places like that were always open, I thought, as I hurried across town, the cold just starting to bite at my feet. When I got there, I realized how naïve I'd been. This wasn't Walton's Mountain where people never locked their front doors. I didn't know what to do. By that time I was exhausted and sick of walking.

The porch was pretty big and inviting, even though it wasn't totally covered and it was almost Halloween. I didn't know what else I could do. There was no way I was going back. I took all the clothes I'd hastily packed and put them on at once. They didn't amount to much, just a sweatshirt and some jeans. I used my pyjama bottoms as a scarf.

Needless to say, I didn't get much sleep. It was freezing cold and I was scared out of my mind. At about five in the morning, when the sun started to rise, I knew there was no point even trying to sleep. I sat up and looked around. It was really quite beautiful at that time of day. There was a hazy mist around the gravestones and the grass twinkled with frost, like it had been sprayed with deodorant.

I stamped my feet and had a bit of a walk around as I munched on a few apples I'd packed for my breakfast. By eight o'clock I was bored and thought about going into town. It was tempting. I could treat myself to a fry-up, but maybe it was too risky. Any one of my family might be out and about at that time.

Eventually a van pulled up, driven by Brian's dad. They'd come to drop off the equipment. I've never been so happy to see anyone in my life. He didn't seem as happy to see me. Apparently my folks had been up all night, phoning all my friends to see where I was. I thought I was avoiding trouble by running away, but had I made things a whole lot worse?

***

If it had been anyone else, I wouldn't have listened, but it was Brian, gorgeous, lovely Brian. He knew I didn't want to go home, but didn't push me to tell him why. He'd heard my dad spill to the whole world that I had a sister who was missing, so I told him all about Ellie over a nice hot breakfast at his house.

He was lovely about it, really sympathetic about my family having been through so much. He said it certainly explained why my dad was overprotective, and even said he'd probably be just the same in his shoes. He kind of made me see it from Dad's perspective and I started to feel sorry for him. I mean, yeah, he went about it totally the wrong way, but his heart was in the right place.

I told Brian that I thought Zara was lucky to have him and he seemed a bit embarrassed. I didn't care though; he was really great to talk to and seemed to know exactly what to say. He spent nearly all day with me and just listened as I told him the whole story of what it's like being a Hunter. I thought about telling him what I'd been doing to myself, but I didn't want him to think I was weird, and anyway, it was my secret.

He escorted me home just before teatime and even went in first to pave the way. Everyone was pleased to see me. They really had been worried, and I felt so bad for what I had put them through. I could tell Dad was still cross, but he didn't have a go at me. I think he was too scared of losing me. Mum sent me straight upstairs for a bath and bed, and I went willingly. I was dead on my feet.

I came downstairs after my bath to say goodnight, but stopped dead in my tracks outside the lounge door. I could hear Lee talking to Mum and Dad about me.

'Are you sure she's not being bullied at school?' Mum asked gently.

'She's fine,' Lee said, sounding irritable. I think he was trying to have a game on his PlayStation.

'So there's nothing we should know? She's got friends and she's happy?' Dad asked.

'She's happy enough mooning around after Brian like a lovesick puppy,' said Lee, 'but not sure about the friends bit, though.' I took a sharp breath and had to be careful not to make a noise to alert them to my presence.

'What do you mean? Zara and Abby seem like nice girls,' I heard Mum say.

'They are … to her face. But you should hear what they say behind her back. She's the school joke.' I couldn't believe what I was hearing. Abby and Zara didn't really hate me, did they?

FIFTEEN

There was no way I ever wanted to go back to school. Everyone knew about Ellie and would be going on about it. I just couldn't face them, especially now I knew they all hated me. I stayed in bed, even though I could hear Mum shouting at me to get up. I buried my head under the pillows and tried to get back to sleep.

I didn't get very far. With dread, I heard Mum running upstairs and knocking on my door. I didn't answer, hoping that she'd go away, though I knew she wouldn't. She came in and sat on the edge of my bed, pulled the cover back a bit and started stroking my hair.

I knew she was looking at me intently and I found it hard to stay still, not even twitch a muscle. I pretended to wake up. I turned over and slowly opened my eyes, giving Mum my best bleary and pathetic look.

It worked, sort of. I could see her eyes soften. I think she was genuinely worried about me. She used her gentle and concerned voice, which was just what I needed. Then she told me it didn't matter if I didn't have many friends. I was furious she had believed what Lee had said, and then I realized I had no right to be. I believed it myself.

Mum let me stay off for the morning and proceeded to make me feel I would have been better off in the pit of vipers called school. I get on fine with Mum, but she was so busy with her two jobs and the hunt for Ellie that she really didn't have a clue about what was going on in my life.

She told me all about having a crush on a boy when she was at school and said that although what I felt seemed like love now, it wasn't. I could have curled up and died. It was bad enough everyone had sussed my feelings for Brian, but then to have Mum be so patronizing about it and tell me it wasn't real, it was too much.

I dragged my heels on the walk to school. I considered not going in at all and taking myself off somewhere for an adventure. But Lee knew I was coming in at lunchtime. Mum had told him to look out for me. I didn't like feeling that everyone was watching out for me. It was far better just being the girl in the background that no one noticed.

* * *

When I arrived, it felt like the whole school stopped talking and turned and looked at me. I saw Lee and Bombhead playing footie with some other lads. Lee pretended he hadn't seen me and carried on with the game, but he was so checking up on me. The tell-tale sign was the ball flying right past his head when he was meant to be in goal.

I made my way through the playground and away from all those prying eyes. I figured if I could just get to the cloakroom, I could hide out in there until the bell went. I wasn't even scared at the prospect of being in there on my own. Maybe the ghost would be good company; maybe she could be my new best friend, seeing as the job was up for grabs.

Unfortunately, and just my luck, it was crowded when I got there, and who should be holding court but Steph. She grinned when she saw me, not 'cos she was pleased to see me, just 'cos I was the source of all that day's gossip. I tried to ignore everyone, just go to my peg, leave my stuff and go into the loos – and stay there forever. Typically, Steph followed me.

'You're a dark horse.' She looked impressed. I smiled weakly and headed for a cubicle, but she stopped me by standing in the way. 'So what's this about a missing sister? Where's she gone? Is she dead or what?'

'If I knew the answer to all that, she wouldn't be missing, would she?' I snapped. Steph pulled a 'sorree' face. Did she really expect me to sit down with her and the girls, and have a merry old chat about it? She didn't ask me any more, just stepped aside and let me go into the cubicle. I locked the door behind me and sat on the closed lid, pulling my knees up to my chest and trying not to cry.

Before I knew it, there she was again, peering over the top of the cubicle from the one next to mine. 'Everyone reckons your dad murdered her. He's a right weirdo the way he never lets you do stuff. Does he hit you? Is that why you're such a weed?' I jumped to my feet and reached for the lock on the door. I was going to have her, I was going to pull her down from her perch and pull her stupid hair out and punch her in the face.

Zara and Abby stopped me. They had just come in and seen what was going on. My heart sank. It could only get worse from here. If Steph was giving me a hard time, then they were going to be twice as bad.

'Leave her alone!' Zara yelled at Steph. I jumped, partly from the sound of Zara's shriek, mostly from the shock of her defending me.

'Yeah, get lost Steph!' warned Abby.

'Just doing my duty for the people,' replied Steph, indicating other girls from our class who had gathered to watch. 'We just want to know the truth once and for all, so we can put an end to all those nasty rumours.' Zara grabbed her and started pushing her out. The crowd dispersed and allowed them through.

'I said, leave her alone!' Zara bellowed in her face.

'Keep your hair on, zit face.' Steph backed away, then sauntered off, taking her posse with her, though not without giving me a sarcastic little wave first.

I should have felt reassured being left alone with Zara and Abby, but it bothered me. Why they were being so nice to me? Zara put her arm around me and asked if I was okay. I nodded, not sure whether to believe her seemingly genuine concern. She led me over to one of the benches and we sat down, Zara and Abby on either side of me, all friendly squeezes and gentle voices. 'What was all this?' I wondered.

'You should have told us about Ellie,' said Abby. It was weird hearing someone else say her name.

'Lee said you've been having a really tough time about it,' added Zara. I snorted with derision. This was all I needed. What else had Lee been saying?

'Any time you want to talk about it …' said Zara. She almost had me believing she could be that sweet.

'Yeah, any time, day or night.' I couldn't believe this. They'd been treating me like a leper since the beginning of term, and now there was some gossip to be had, they were all over me like a rash. I felt angry. They were so transparent. I didn't need them; I didn't need anybody.

'Thanks,' I grabbed my stuff and got up to leave, 'but I'd rather drink acid than tell you two anything that means anything to me.' They looked shocked and stung. 'Did you really think I'd fall for this *we're your best friends* routine?' They looked back at me with blank faces. I could see Zara was starting to get angry, but I wasn't scared. I didn't care if I never spoke to her again.

Zara stood up and came towards me. 'Why would we want to hang around with a geek like you from your weirdo family. We were only being nice to you 'cos Brian asked us to. And while I'm on the subject, stay away from my boyfriend!'

Her nose was inches from mine, but I glared right back at her. I had stuff to be angry about, too. 'Come on,' she said grabbing Abby's arm. 'Let's leave the loser alone.' With that, she had flung the door open and disappeared. I didn't feel so brave any more and my legs started to shake beneath me.

I ran back into one of the cubicles and locked myself in. There was no way I was going to risk anyone seeing me cry. I stayed there for a long time. The only thing that calmed me down was picking at the new scab on my arm where I had cut myself with Dad's razor.

* * *

When I eventually ventured out, the corridors were all empty, as the bell hadn't yet gone. I hurried to wait outside the classroom for my next lesson, hoping that my absence hadn't been noted from the one before. I was glad it was Maths and I wasn't in the same set as Zara and Abby.

The bell rang and suddenly I felt swamped by hundreds of people all around me. I grabbed a seat at the back of the room and kept my head down. I could tell my classmates were still talking about me and I didn't want eye contact with any of them.

Brian dashed into the room before the teacher arrived. He came and sat next to me. I was confused by what he was doing there. He was in the top set for Maths.

'Can I have a word?' he whispered, breathless. He might as well have used a loudspeaker, as everyone fell silent and turned to listen. He glared at them all, then grabbed me by the arm and led me out into the corridor, making sure he shut the door behind him.

'Are you okay?'

'Not you as well.' I was sick of people asking me.

'Sorry,' he said, and I felt bad I'd hurt his feelings. Just then, Mr Cookson rounded the corner and wanted to know what we were doing. Brian thought on his feet and put his arm around me. He told Mr Cookson I was feeling ill and needed to go to the nurse. Mr Cookson nodded and away we went.

He took me to our form room, knowing it would be quiet there.

'So how are you … really?' he asked.

'Hasn't Zara told you?' I felt sure she would have run back to him and told him not to bother with me.

'I haven't seen her since lunch.'

'I had a go at her,' I told him. 'She and Abby were all over me and I know they don't like me that much really.' It was out there before I knew what I was saying.

''Course they do,' he said, trying to make light of it.

'She told me you asked her to be nice to me.'

'Oh.' Neither of us knew what to say next and I took the silence to mean it was the end of the conversation.

I got up to leave. Brian grabbed me by the wrist and made me sit down again, this time a lot closer to him.

'I was just worried about you. I'll talk to her. She'll understand you were just upset. You've had a tough time of it.'

I looked down. He still hadn't let go of me. He was using his thumb to stroke my inner wrist. It felt warm and exciting, like electricity was rushing into my body from his. I didn't pull away and he stroked me some more. His face turned to curiosity as he looked down. I followed his gaze and saw he was looking at my plasters.

'Have you hurt yourself?' he asked. I snatched my arm away, the spell broken.

'No,' I lied. 'It's nothing.'

Brian kept his distance after that. I could tell by the way he looked at me that he was still worried, but I couldn't risk talking to him, not if he was going to start asking me about my cuts. It was almost the end of term and I couldn't wait for the holidays. Just a few more days of the hell that had become school and then I'd be free, or so I thought.

I'd noticed Lee and Brian had become pretty pally over the past few weeks. It bugged me. I felt like Lee had swanned into my social circle at school and stolen all my friends. He'd been getting off with Abby at every opportunity and I knew it wouldn't be long before he asked her out.

Zara, Abby and Steph hadn't spoken to me since the day I blew up at them all. I didn't like it much, but I got used to being on my own. If one good thing was coming out of all this, it was that I was doing really well with my grades. I didn't want to look like a drop kick by having lunch on my own, so I started taking a packed lunch into the library.

One day, when I was getting changed for P.E., Zara made a big deal about announcing she and Brian were going to do it over the Christmas holidays. I got the feeling she was saying it for my benefit, but I just thought she looked sad. I felt sad for Brian, too. If she really cared about him, she wouldn't go around telling the whole world about intimate stuff like that.

I did my best to ignore her, but in retrospect that made her worse. She was determined to get a rise out of me. The hockey pitch was freezing cold and the air was damp and icy. If there was one place on earth I really didn't want to be, it was out there with a load of bitches on a December afternoon.

Luckily, I was last to be picked and got the place on my team no one else wanted. It was fine by me. I'd just hang back and keep myself to myself and run the other way if a ball came near me. Mrs Mitchell soon wised up to what I was doing and made an example of me by telling me the whole point of my position was to defend. It felt as though everyone was sniggering at me.

Soon Zara came running towards me. She was covering Claire, who was just about to score a goal. While everyone else was either cheering or groaning, Zara took the chance to have a dig at me.

'You didn't seriously think you could steal Brian off me, did you?' she sneered.

'I wouldn't want to,' I replied. God, she was up herself.

'Not what I heard,' she said, before running off to tackle the ball from Sarah Bell.

She won the ball of course and then she was heading for me again. Her eyes looked hungry, like a salivating dog's. She got closer and closer, and I heard all my teammates screaming at me to run forward and stop her from getting a goal. The look in Zara's eyes warned me not to even try and I was happy not to. Who cared about hockey anyway?

Then Mrs Mitchell got involved. She was running along the side of the pitch with the whistle in her mouth, demonstrating with her hockey stick what I should do. I half-heartedly jogged towards Zara, looking her in the eye and getting ready to bar her way.

Her eyes darkened and hardened. She expertly stopped the ball and lifted her stick to give it an almighty whack. In that split second, I saw my opportunity and went to swipe the ball from underneath her. She was too fast for me, and her stick came crashing down. It was only when a searing pain shot through my ankle that I realized she'd never intended it for the ball.

* * *

It hurt like hell, but I was glad in a way. I was starting to get a real taste for pain. I made out to Mrs Mitchell that it was a lot worse than it was. She seemed concerned and excused me from the rest of the lesson. I went to the locker room to change, happy that I could be out of there before the others had even finished the game.

Mum was away, following up another lead about Ellie, so I went into town after school. I knew none of the others would be back for ages. I went into Boots to get some aspirin. My ankle had swollen and was starting to turn purple around the bone. It was making me feel light-headed and queasy.

I wasn't in any hurry and wandered around in there aimlessly. I didn't need anything other than painkillers, but I felt like I needed a treat. Then it hit me. I rounded the corner and there were rows and rows of nail scissors, tweezers and lash curlers. I knew in that moment that my own scissors were my treat. I'd make up a box just for cutting, and in it I'd keep all the tools I needed.

I suddenly had a purpose and felt my skin tingle with excitement as I grabbed a basket. It took me ages to choose from all the varieties of cotton wool, antiseptic cream and plasters. I was just about to take my booty to the till and pay, when a load of neatly rolled bandages wrapped in wax paper caught my eye.

I felt like a naughty kid. I mean, little nicks here and there were nothing, but could I ever cut myself so I'd need a bandage? It felt like a challenge. I bit my lip with anticipation as I reached out for one. I didn't intend to use it, but I'd keep it, just in case.

***

No one was in when I got home. I felt bitter when I thought about Lee out having a great time with Zara, Abby and Brian, but it didn't take me long to talk myself into thinking I was far better off than them. I had something secret that they'd never even dreamed of: I had cutting.

I rummaged through all the junk at the bottom of my wardrobe, looking for the perfect box. Shoe boxes were too big, jewellery boxes too small. I knew in my head exactly what I was looking for, but I couldn't find it there. Then I remembered one of Dan's mates had given him a small timber box of cigars for his 18th. I headed straight for his room and found it under the bed. He'd never miss it.

Back in my room, I felt really excited. I put some music on and sat on the floor, taking all my new purchases out of their packaging and laying them out in front of me. I was disappointed when they didn't all fit in the box at first, but with some careful rearranging, they soon did, and they looked so beautiful and inviting.

So inviting. I took the scissors out and wondered if I had ever seen anything more beautiful. I wasn't going to cut myself, I felt too happy. But I held the blades against my skin; I just wanted to know how it felt. The phone rang downstairs and I let the machine get it. I was having too much fun. But then, before I knew what was happening, Lee had burst into my room, thrusting the phone at me.

For a split second, I thought he hadn't noticed and then I saw him clock my box of delights and, what's more, the bottle of aspirin lying on the floor. There was no way he could have a go at me. There were three of us in the room: him, me and whoever was on the phone. I indicated for him to get lost, glad that the call would give me enough time to come up with an explanation.

'Hello,' I said, wondering who it was. I never got calls any more. Nothing. 'Hello?' I repeated, thinking it might be Mum on a dodgy line. But the giggles that came down the line before it was slammed down told me it wasn't her at all. I knew who it was. I threw the phone across the room, cursing them for how miserable they were making me.

I heard Lee coming back upstairs and shoved everything into my school bag, rolled my sleeves down and tried to look like everything was okay. He burst back in to my room and came straight over to me.

'What were you doing?'

'When?' I said nonchalantly, feigning innocence.

'Just then!' he barked.

'What *are* you on about?' If there was any way I could make him think he'd imagined it, I was desperate enough to go for it.

'I saw you.' He looked around the room and started to go through my stuff. I grabbed things out of his hands. This was such an invasion of my privacy.

'You don't know what you saw,' I spat back at him.

'It doesn't take a genius!'

'Oh, get lost!' I pushed him out of the room. He was a lot stronger and fought his way back inside. He grabbed me by the shoulders and shook me.

'Have you taken something?' he screamed in my face. 'Just tell me now and I'll get you to hospital.' I laughed in his face as cruelly as I could.

'Yeah, I have,' I said smiling, enjoying how white he went. 'Your bitch of a girlfriend's mate nearly broke my ankle in hockey this afternoon!' I pulled my sock down and showed him my amazing new bruise. 'I took a couple of aspirin. Is that okay with you?'

I could tell he felt stupid and I was pleased my plan had worked. He left the room quietly. It was only then that I started to shake. That was really way too close, I thought to myself as I slid down my closed bedroom door and started to cry.

SEVENTEEN

Mum got back on the day before we broke up. She was gutted she hadn't managed to find Ellie, not even a sniff of her. Her mood seemed to bring the whole family down. We'd all been secretly imagining how brilliant it would have been to have her back for Christmas. It felt grim knowing that wasn't going to happen. Was being stuck in the house with my miserable family for days on end going to be any better than going to school?

The last day was a bit of an ordeal. I thought it would be a doddle as we were allowed to wear our own clothes and watch videos in lessons. It started to go wrong when Zara and her mates started taking the mick out of what I was wearing. As far as I could see it wasn't that different from any of their outfits, but they were never happy unless they were finding fault with something.

We were having a proper sit-down Christmas dinner. I got mine and went and sat with some other kids in my class, but then the weirdest thing happened. Lee, who had been wishing he was joined at the hip to Abby for weeks now, came and sat with me instead of her. Then, to top it off, Brian came and joined us. Abby and Zara, who were holding court at another table on the other side of the hall, did not look happy.

I enjoyed it for a moment, until Brian and Lee both started acting weird with me. They were being way too friendly, pretending they were interested in everything I said and smiling at me all the time. It really put me on edge. It didn't last long, though. Zara and Abby obviously couldn't stand not knowing what we were talking about, so they grabbed their plates and came to join us.

The atmosphere immediately changed and no one knew what to say. I just stared at my plate and played with my food. Suddenly I'd lost my appetite.

'So how come this table was so interesting?' Zara asked Brian after a few minutes. 'It's hardly party atmosphere, is it?' Brian shrugged. He obviously didn't want to get into a discussion with her about it. Something was up. Maybe it was just wishful thinking, but I could have sworn things weren't that good between him and Zara. He seemed tense when she was around and if you looked really close at his eyes (as I was in the habit of doing), you could tell her voice was grating on his nerves.

Zara grabbed one of the party-poppers that the dinner ladies had put out on the tables for us. She grinned as she set it off in my direction, intending it to hit me full in the face as it did. I ignored her. Brian sighed and gave her a withering look. She didn't take too kindly to that and peeled Abby away from Lee. Together they sauntered off. Lee excused himself and went after them, leaving me and Brian alone.

'Sorry about her,' he said.

'I'm used to it.' He smiled at me and looked at me really intensely. It made me blush and I had to look away.

'So, how have you been?' he asked.

'All right.'

'It's just that Lee told me he thought you were a bit down.'

'Did he now? What else has he been telling you?' I was bristling now. How dare Lee talk about me, to Brian of all people? I had to get to the bottom of how much he knew. My whole secret was in jeopardy.

'He's worried you might be tempted to do something stupid,' he said.

'Like what?' I asked, deliberately playing dumb.

'Look, I think we both know what I'm talking about here!' he said, growing a bit impatient.

'Enlighten me.' I felt more than a little indignant.

He looked around to make sure absolutely no one could hear, or even lip-read. Then he leaned forward and lowered his voice even more. 'He thinks you were trying to top yourself.' I snorted. It was a gut reaction. 'He says he walked into your room and you were cutting yourself with a pair of scissors.' I gulped, trying to keep my cool. So Lee had seen after all.

'I don't have to listen to this.' I tried to sound as outraged as I could. 'Anyway, it's none of your business!' I tried to walk off, but he grabbed me.

'Sit down, Lisa,' he said calmly. I glared at him. I wasn't going to have him boss me around. 'Sit down!' I'd never seen him angry before. I was so shocked, I just did as I was told. 'Now listen. You've really scared Lee. Did you know he's hardly slept since that day 'cos he's been so worried about you?' I gave him a *yeah, right* look. I found that very hard to believe.

'I can help you ...' he whispered, '... if you'll let me?'

It had been so long since anyone was this nice to me I didn't know how to handle it. He looked so sincere that for a moment I thought about telling him. For a moment, I wondered if he really would understand. Then reality came crashing back in. Of course he wouldn't. No one would. I was a freak. Who else would deliberately cut themselves?

* * *

I got out of having to confide in him pretty well, even though there was part of me that wanted to. I thanked him for his concern and told him there really was nothing to worry about. All I had to do was go home and rip Lee's head off for blabbing about me and then that would be an end to it, or so I thought.

I think Lee knew he'd done something wrong, 'cos when I finally caught up with him, he was all sweetness and light to me.

'All right, sis?' he said, a nervous smile streaking his face.

'No, actually,' I said. I was finding it hard to speak at all, I was so angry. 'What did you go and tell Brian for?'

'I was worried about you.' He sounded indignant. Maybe he really did think he'd done the right thing.

'So how come you didn't talk to me about it then?'

'You wouldn't let me. You screamed at me and chucked me out of your room, remember?'

'I could kill you sometimes. Why him of all people?'

'It's not like you've got loads of friends to choose from. And anyhow, he knows about stuff like that.'

'Stuff like what?' Lee went quiet. He'd realized he'd said too much. My instinct told me he'd led me into some place he'd rather I wasn't. 'Like what?' I yelled. This time it was so loud I even made myself jump.

'Cutting!' he yelled back. We were both shocked into silence. I wasn't sure if I wanted to hear any more. It was too much for me to process. It was my secret. I'd hugged it all to myself for weeks and weeks and I liked it there. Now there was a real danger that the whole world could find out if Lee didn't keep his mouth shut.

'I hate you!' I shrieked as I lunged at him, and I really meant it. I hit him as hard as I could and we fell onto the floor. He curled up with his fists around his head, trying to protect himself, but then he got angry too and started lashing out at me. He's much stronger than I am, and as we tussled on the floor, we rolled into the Christmas tree and nearly brought it down on top of us.

'What the hell's going on?' We were so busy yelling and kicking, we hadn't heard Mum come in from late-night shopping. She pulled Lee off me and threw him onto the sofa. I sat up, crying by this stage. 'What's got into you two?' she demanded.

'Ask her,' said Lee sulkily. Mum looked at me with expectation. There was no way I was going to tell her what this was all about. I got up and tried to leg it to my room. Mum stopped me and made me sit on the sofa next to Lee.

'Neither of you is going anywhere until you tell me what this is all about,' she shouted. I stayed silent and glared at Lee, willing him to do the same.

'Tell her,' he said, glaring back at me. I shook my head.

'Tell me what?' asked Mum with dread. She obviously thought I'd got into some kind of trouble at school.

'Nothing,' I said.

'Tell me what?' Lee looked at me, and at that moment I knew there was nothing I could do to stop him.

'Lisa cuts herself!' he blurted. I felt like I was trapped in a void. I could hear and see what was going on around me, but I couldn't react to it. What I wanted to do was run and scream, but my legs wouldn't work and I'd lost my voice.

'What do you mean?' asked Mum, confused. Lee was shaking at this point. He looked really upset.

'Look at her arms, Mum. Look at her arms!' Before I knew what was happening, she was grabbing at me and pulling my sleeves up. I didn't even have the strength to resist.

'Oh, Lisa,' she said when she saw my pretty patterns. 'What have you done?' And then she started to cry.

* * *

Mum phoned the doctor first thing the next day and I got dragged down to the surgery before I'd even had a chance to have breakfast. It was a horrible, embarrassing experience and one I never want to repeat. Mum was a total wreck and in the end the doctor had to tell her to wait outside so he could talk to me alone.

He was old and stuffy, and asked me why I'd been hurting myself like that. I just shrugged. I didn't want to talk to anyone about it, especially not an old goat like him. He did say that other people hurt themselves and I'd be surprised by how many. I knew he was just trying to be nice, but I really didn't want to be put in the same category as head-cases.

He told me he thought it would be a good idea if I went to see a counsellor for a bit. I wanted to cry when he said that. I knew everyone thought I was mad. How was I going to tell Mum about this? She had so much to worry about already, and Dad would just hit the roof.

He doesn't believe in stuff like that. He thinks it's all Americanized rubbish – stiff upper lip and all that.

* * *

The rest of the Christmas holidays turned out to be a nightmare. I had no privacy and I even got followed to the loo. I knew Mum had told Dan and Dad about what had happened and Dan was really sweet and had a nice chat with me about it. Dad, on the other hand, buried his head in his bottle of whiskey as he always does and pretended it wasn't happening.

Christmas Day itself is always a stressful event in our house. Everyone gets maudlin 'cos Ellie's presents stay under the tree unopened. We were all wondering where she was and who she was with; if she was thinking about us too, if she was even still alive, but it was Mum who got particularly upset that year.

She was bristling and snappy over dinner. We tried to have the best time we could, but it was pretty hard with the amount Dad was drinking. She kept looking at me funny all day, as if she was just about to say something and had then thought better of it. But then, as we were clearing up, she just went mad and yelled at me.

'I just want to know why, Lisa?' she demanded. It came, as if from nowhere.

'Know what?' I asked weakly, a feeling of dread leaking into the pit of my stomach. I suspected I knew what she was on about.

'Why do that to yourself? What's wrong with you?' Good question, I thought, knowing it wasn't the time or place for irony. 'Don't you think there's enough going on in this house without you putting pressure on us, too?' My eyes prickled and I knew I was going to cry. 'What is it? Some kind of attention-seeking or something?'

I was startled. She'd been so nice and supportive when I'd told her about the counsellor, and now she was yelling at me as if I'd deliberately done it to upset her or something.

'Well, it's worked.' She looked furious. 'You've got our attention. Happy flaming Christmas everyone!' She had a weird glint in her eye. Thankfully, Dad had fallen asleep. Dan and Lee came in to calm her down. They looked at her like she'd gone mad. I took the chance to leg it up to my room. I couldn't hack it. It wasn't just that she was attacking me for something I had no control over, but attacking me in front of everyone. I thought she understood.

Looking back, I think she had so much to worry about that she just exploded. I just wished it hadn't been at me. It was pretty scary being me that Christmas. I didn't have a clue what was happening in my *own* head, let alone in Mum's.

EIGHTEEN

I kept out of Mum's way for the next few days. She kept wanting to 'talk' and she must have apologized a hundred times. She said she lost it 'cos she thought she was the only one thinking of Ellie over Christmas and that the rest of us had forgotten about her. She'd had a long talk with Dad and he'd made her see that we all miss her, it's just that we show it in different ways.

Even so, I couldn't forget all the nasty things she'd said just like that. If she could snap once, she could do it again, and I didn't want to be close enough to be in the line of fire. I think it got her down a bit that I was acting distant. It wasn't just her, though. I didn't really want to be alone with any of my family – I knew they'd only take it as an opportunity to *mend* me, as if it would be that easy.

I spent most of the holidays hanging out in my room. I got used to being on my own. I kind of liked it that way; it felt safe. I sound like a spod, but I got all my homework and coursework out of the way. I knew if Zara, Abby or any of the others at school found out, they'd tease me like hell, but I was just banking on Lee not telling them. It wasn't like I just locked myself away for the whole holidays swotting. I did other stuff, too.

Mum had put a diary in my stocking. I get one every year. When we were kids, Lee and Dan would get football ones and me and Ellie would get a J17 one each. I sat on my bed on New Year's Eve afternoon listening to one of my new CDs and filling in my personal details on the first page. It looked neat and unspoilt, and gave me hope for the year ahead. I decided to make a list of New Year's resolutions; I wanted this year to be different.

1. Find Ellie.
2. Stop cutting.
3. Stop obsessing about Brian and get my own boyfriend.

I was chewing on the end of my pen and considering adding more when there was a knock on my bedroom door. I looked up and Dan poked his head in. My heart sank. Did he still think he had to check up on me, or was this for yet another tête-à-tête?

'Someone's here to see you,' he said. I was puzzled. Who'd call round for me? Dan stepped aside to reveal Brian standing behind him, smiling awkwardly and wringing his scarf in his hands. My stomach lurched at the sight of him, all polite and gentle. I slammed the diary shut on my resolutions. It had taken me all of five seconds to break number three.

Dan went back downstairs, deliberately leaving the door open. Did he really think I was going to jump on someone else's boyfriend and start having rampant sex or something? It felt weird having Brian in my bedroom. It was almost too intimate.

'I just wondered if you might fancy a walk?' he asked. It did sound tempting, but I was wary. I got the feeling he'd only called round to lecture me, just like my family.

'But if you're busy …' he said, eyeing the closed diary in my lap. I think he could sense my hesitation.

'Where are you thinking of going?' I was hoping to buy myself a bit more time while I decided whether it was a good idea.

'Just to the park.' I don't think he realized it would be such hard work to persuade me. 'Maybe a pizza afterwards, if you'd like?'

'I'll come …' I told him, '… but I can't stay out long.' I didn't have anything else to do that day, but that was my get-out clause in case things got too heavy.

'Don't worry about your dad,' Brian offered. 'I spoke to him downstairs and asked if it would be okay to take you out. He said as long as I get you back as soon after midnight as I can, then he and your mum are fine with it.' It was almost too much for me to take in all at once. How come Mum and Dad were so cool all of a sudden and did Brian really use the phrase *take you out*? As in a *date*?

Conversation didn't come that easy at first. I asked him how Zara was and his reply was monosyllabic. I was really sure something was up between them. I wanted to ask, but I couldn't find the words. Something about him was different, but I couldn't put my finger on what it was. I'd been so worried he'd want to talk about cutting, but he didn't even mention it once. He seemed distracted and preoccupied.

When we got to the edge of the park, I suggested we get some food. I was starving. We tried to get into Pizza Hut and Bella Pasta, but they were fully booked – it was New Year's Eve, after all. Brian seemed mortified that he hadn't thought of booking. I told him it was no big deal, but he still seemed pensive.

We shared a bag of chips and walked through a grave-yard. It was dark and cold, but it wasn't scary and Brian wrapped his scarf around me. Something had changed between us. I knew he had something on his mind and it was bothering him. I wanted him to talk to me. It felt nice being the supportive one for a change, 'cos usually it's the whole world asking me if I'm okay.

It was getting late when he told me what was up. We were sitting on a bench by the side of the church and my hands were tingling with cold. Brian's expression was so serious it made me giggle.

'I don't want to be with Zara any more …' he said. My head started spinning, but before I'd worked out what I should say, he carried on. '… I want to be with you,' he finished, taking one of my hands in his. I was dumb-struck. Was this really happening? And then he kissed me. Brian Drake kissed me on the stroke of midnight, and for a while, everything seemed perfect.

* * *

I didn't see Brian the next day as he had to go and visit relatives, and then the day after that I had my first appointment with the counsellor. I'd spent most of the holidays trying to think up a way to get out of it. I acted as normally as I could, trying to prove to my family it had all been a blip and I didn't need help after all. Why would I want to talk to a perfect stranger about it anyway? It was in the past now. I didn't need help any more. I had Brian and I was happy.

Dan caught me trying to cancel and made me put the phone down. I've never felt more like a child. I tried to explain to him that I really didn't need to go, but he reck-oned I did. I begged and pleaded with him to talk to Mum and Dad, but he was on their side and there was nothing I could do to change his mind. I tried reasoning with him, I tried yelling at him, but in the middle of it all, Mum came home from work to pick me up.

'Ready?' she said breezily, though I could tell she was just as nervous as I was. I looked at Dan. This was his last chance to save me – if he wanted to. Of course, he didn't, and Mum and I drove there in silence.

It wasn't half as bad as I'd expected. I thought I'd be taken into a stark room where I'd have to lie down and talk about myself while some fusty old man looked at me curiously over half-moon glasses, occasionally nodding and taking notes. Instead, a woman called Rachel came and got me from reception. She looked too young to be a counsellor, but I was glad; rather that than a coffin-dodger.

We went into a small room with a few plants, a few books, two comfy chairs and a box of tissues. The tissues made me nervous. Was it a foregone conclusion that I was going to cry? I didn't want to cry, but what if that was what was expected? My stomach tightened and I felt tense as I waited for her to start grilling me.

'Don't worry,' she said. 'You look terrified.'

'I am,' I confided. She seemed amused and I must admit I did feel pretty dumb. She wasn't scary at all. She asked me about my Christmas, what presents I'd got, how I was getting on at school – that kind of thing. The only thing to distinguish it from any other chat with someone I'd just met for the first time was that she was taking notes, but not many, and she said I could read them if I wanted to. I didn't. I trusted her straightaway. She wasn't nosy at all and didn't make me talk about anything that I hadn't brought into the conversation myself. I was glad she didn't ask me about cutting. I didn't want to talk about it … not yet.

When I came out, Mum looked even more anxious than when I went in. She seemed surprised that I was quite chirpy and kept looking at me oddly. It was only when the car was pulling out of the car park that she asked me how it went. I told her it was fine and smiled to confirm it. Her sigh of relief was audible.

* * *

I felt a lot more confident about going back to school. I was hoping Zara and Abby would have moved on to picking on someone else, but if they hadn't, I didn't care. I had Brian and I had Rachel. I knew for sure they both liked me.

It was snowing outside, so we were all in our form room for first break. Zara and Abby were hogging the radiator and speaking in hushed tones. Zara looked like she'd been crying and I wondered, no, I hoped it was because Brian had chucked her. He'd had to go and talk to Miss Capshaw about his music coursework or something. I was desperate for him to arrive. When he did, my whole body tingled.

I monitored Zara to see how she reacted to his arrival. She certainly didn't look like she hated him. In fact, she looked quite plaintive, which was really not like her. When Abby saw him, she came rushing over, whispered something in his ear, then dragged him by the sleeve over to the radiator.

I watched them all closely. Zara was crying again and Brian had his arm around her, although he looked like he really wasn't enjoying it. Something big was going on and I didn't have a clue what it was. A few minutes later the bell went. I got my books together for Geography, but I couldn't peel my eyes off what was going on by the window. Zara and Abby sauntered past. I tried to pretend I wasn't looking, but I wasn't quick enough.

'Bitch!' spat Abby, linking her arm through Zara's. I realized they must know about Brian and me. I did feel bad for taking him off her, but then he made a move on me, not the other way around. I didn't say anything. I didn't want to get into a fight with them on the first day back, and anyway, they didn't hang around long enough for a reply.

Brian came over as soon as the coast was clear. 'Sorry about that.'

'Don't worry,' I told him. 'I think I'd be pretty upset if my boyfriend dumped me for the girl I hated most in the school.' Brian looked away from me and my heart sank. I knew instantly that he hadn't had the heart to do it. Hadn't he meant it when he told me he wanted to be with me? He saw how gutted I was and lifted my face gently in his hand. I had no choice but to look at him.

'Listen to me,' he said in a tone that was more forceful than usual. 'Nothing's changed. I still feel exactly the same about you.' I felt the heat in my cheeks, and pleasure fluttering in my tummy. 'It's just it's really not a good time for Zara. I can't finish with her at the moment.'

'Why not?' I knew my voice sounded whiney. Surely the longer he left it, the less likely he was to do it, and anyway, when is a good time to chuck someone?

'You don't know, do you?' he asked and I shook my head. What was going on? 'Adam's been in a car crash. He might not make it.' I was shocked. As it sank in, I couldn't help asking myself how I was supposed to react to news like that about the girl who'd done nothing but make my life hell all of last term. Brian asked me if I understood why he couldn't do it and I remember nodding. I felt numb and full of dread. My optimism for the New Year drained away as I watched him hurry off to comfort her.

NINETEEN

It was miserable getting up for school that term. Even with the heating on full blast, the house was cold and it was dark outside while we were having breakfast. I'd shiver getting undressed for the shower, but at least I got up early enough to get in there first. The water never usually lasts for five hot showers in a row, so if you went in last, like Lee did most days, it was unbearably cold.

One Tuesday morning, I'd slept in a bit. I'd stayed up late the night before, talking to Brian on my mobile. Dan was in the bathroom and Mum was banging on the door for him to hurry up, so I decided to have breakfast first while there was a queue. The post had just plopped onto the mat and I picked it up, yawning. I don't even know why I bothered to look through it. There was never anything for me.

I was just about to throw it onto the counter in the kitchen and help myself to some cornflakes when my brain seemed to catch up with my eyes. I was sure I'd seen a Spanish stamp on one of the envelopes. I picked the bundle up again. I was right. There it was, a card with what looked like Ellie's writing on it. I was freaked. I stared at it. Was my mind playing tricks on me?

Dan came down in just a towel. Looking at him with wet hair made me shudder and snuggle myself deeper into my hooded dressing-gown. He ignored me as he does most mornings, but my absolute silence must have alerted him to something as he spun round for no apparent reason and looked at me intently.

'What's up with you?' he demanded while pouring himself some milk. I just looked at him. What should I say – 'Morning Dan, here's a letter from our long-lost sister'? I felt like an animal caught in headlights and I started shaking. Then Dan got really worried and before I'd managed to dig my voice out of my dry throat, he was feeling my head for a temperature.

'I'm not ill.' I pushed the envelope across the break-fast bar to him. He looked confused at first, like he couldn't add all the pieces up. 'Whose writing does that look like?' I asked. Suddenly it all seemed to make sense to him. He gulped and I saw goose pimples rise up on his flesh. 'What shall we do?' I said. It was addressed to all of us, but it didn't seem right to open it without Mum and Dad.

We called them downstairs. Mum started shaking like I had when she saw the writing. Dad took it out of her hands and ripped it open. I wanted to tell him to be careful; this was the only piece of Ellie we'd had since she went missing and he was destroying it in front of our eyes.

It turned out to be a Christmas card, a very late Christmas card. All it said inside was *Happy Christmas love E*. I was disappointed it didn't say more. We all were. None of us knew what to make of it. We couldn't quite believe that, if it really was from her, she wouldn't have said more after not being in touch for so long. Didn't she have anything else to say to us apart from to let us know she was alive? What did it mean?

Dan got angry. He always thought Ellie was selfish and the thought that she could be so casual made him crazy. The only thing in his mind that made any sense was that it was a joke. He thought someone in Ibiza had seen one of the fliers Mum handed out over there and thought it would be a laugh to send a Christmas card. Yeah right, ha ha.

After a few weeks of relative peace in the house, the arguments suddenly flared up again. Dad had been quite good at staying off the booze since Christmas, but now he was right back where he was before, spending every lunchtime and almost every night in the pub – sometimes he wouldn't come home at all. How could a Christmas card dredge up so much misery and turmoil?

* * *

Brian was worth waiting for; I knew that, so I decided to be patient. He was a good person for sticking by Zara and any jealousy I had about him spending time with her and not me, I tried to squash. She wasn't at school for a while. We heard things were pretty bleak for her brother and the whole family was keeping a bedside vigil at the hospital. Just when the teacher told us all to expect the worst, he came out of his coma and stabilized. It wasn't long before Zara was back at school.

Abby was chuffed she was back. She'd been like a lost puppy while she was away and even Lee had started to get annoyed with her. Zara held court at registration and told most of our class, who had crowded around her, what had happened to her brother. I was sending Brian a text message, and only half listening, when I realized that Zara had stopped talking and was glaring at me. I looked up, wishing I'd heard whatever she'd just said, but the bell rang and she and her cronies walked off.

Just as I was heading off to Art, Brian grabbed me and pulled me into the locker room for a snog. I loved it when he did that and we were both enjoying keeping our relationship secret. When we'd stopped kissing, he told me to watch out as, apparently, the car Zara's brother had crashed in had just been serviced in Dad's garage and she was blaming my whole family, saying we were crooks.

I thanked him for warning me and went to my lesson with a heavy heart. If there was one thing Zara was good at, it was making me feel bad, and now it seemed she had a good reason. I tried to sit as far away from them as possible in Art, but we were doing still life, so we all had to sit around the same bowl of fruit. I couldn't concentrate 'cos she glared at me for the whole lesson. Abby kept whispering things in her ear.

I was glad when the bell rang and deliberately took a long time packing my things away. I thought I was the last one in the room when I went to put my board and clips back in the cupboard, but then I heard a thud behind me. Everything went black and there was the unmistakable sound of Zara and Abby laughing on the other side of the door.

'That'll teach her,' I heard Zara say as the key turned in the lock.

I waited until I was sure they'd gone and then knocked on the door. Mrs Amos was sure to hear me. Or had they been clever enough to get her out of the way first? I certainly couldn't hear any signs of imminent rescue. To make things worse, I knew my bag was only a few metres away, on the other side of the door. If only I had it with me then I could text Brian, and he could save me and no one would ever have to know.

Realizing I might be in for a long wait, I sat on the floor. My eyes had accustomed themselves to the lack of light and my nose seemed extra sensitive. There was a chalky, painty feeling hanging heavily in the air and it caught in the back of my throat. Part of me wanted to curl up and go to sleep.

A glint in an old ice-cream box caught my eye. I couldn't make out what it was at first and then I realized it was the blades for the scalpel knives. My heart skipped a beat. To be locked in a cupboard by a cow like Zara Morgan was one thing, but to be in there with such temptation was quite another. If I could just touch one, hold it in my hands, then maybe it would calm me, I reasoned, as I reached my hand out and dipped it into the box.

None of the blades was especially sharp, but they still felt good as I squeezed my fingers around them. I knew I couldn't go too far while at school, so I picked just one and put the others back. At first I just used the point to dig into my arm a bit. It was like Zara was an insect that had bitten me and I was just scratching the itch.

The thing is, I scratched so hard it bled. My blood looked black in the dim light and I liked it even more. It was like I'd turned on a tap to let all the muck out of me. A few moments later I heard some of the A level students coming in. I licked my new cut to tidy it up and rolled the sleeves of my shirt and jumper over it, knowing they'd be crusty by the time I got home. I shouted for them to let me out, and they did, staring at me like I was crazy.

I turned up almost half an hour late for History and when I did, Zara and Abby exploded into laughter. I don't think they'd expected their plan to go so well. Brian could tell I was upset and looked worried. He indicated for me to come and sit next to him, so I headed over. Unfortunately for me, Mr Byers didn't appreciate tardiness and made me sit at the front of the class for the rest of the lesson, then kept me back afterwards to have a go at me. Not only that, I got a detention, too. Thanks, Zara.

* * *

Brian was desperate to find out what was going on. I didn't want to say it was Zara 'cos I knew he'd excuse her and say maybe I should, too. I told him that things were still a bit weird at home after Ellie's card. Half of me figured if Zara could use her family hassles to get sympathy from him, then so could I.

I went to counselling alone that afternoon. Mum was trying to save up for another trip to look for Ellie and couldn't afford to take the time off work. Rachel asked how everything was going. I didn't tell her about being locked in the art cupboard. I didn't want her to think I was a sap, too.

I wasn't in the mood for talking, but I wanted to be helped. I wished she could just give me a cuddle or something, that someone would just show me unconditional love. I felt stupid for thinking it; I wasn't a kid anymore.

She didn't ask me anything specific, just really general open questions, and if I didn't want to talk, then she didn't push me. The thing was, I think part of me wanted to be pushed. I wanted her to make me think about stuff I didn't understand and help me find some answers, but that whole area was too scary to venture into alone.

I got a bit impatient with her. I didn't know what was wrong, so how was I meant to know how to put it right? That was *her* job, wasn't it? She picked up on my tone and said my body language was closed to her, whatever that means.

'I get the impression you're angry with me, Lisa,' she said. I shrugged, but I didn't know why. She looked at me for a while, waiting for me to elaborate, but I just looked at my shoes. I wanted to be out of there.

'Can I go now?' She looked at the clock. There were still twenty minutes to go.

'Isn't there anything else you want to talk about?' I shrugged again. 'Tell me about your dreams,' she said. I hadn't been expecting that and wondered what the hell they had to do with anything. Then I remembered I'd dreamt of Ellie the night we'd got her card. I couldn't remember all the details and it frustrated me.

'I had one the other night about my sister,' I started. 'We were trying to cross a motorway and I was really scared. I wanted her to hold my hand, but she wouldn't. Every time I put my hand in hers, she pulled it free.'

'Go on,' Rachel said. She was taking notes now.

'I was upset 'cos I felt scared and I didn't understand why she didn't want to comfort me. There were cars whizzing past us really fast and Ellie was looking at them not at me.' I closed my eyes. It was all a bit hazy. Rachel said it didn't matter, just to tell her anything I could remember.

'So she kept pulling her hand free of mine. Then the next time I tried to hold on to her, I looked up and she was gone. She'd run across all the lanes of the motorway and was walking towards a hill.' I could feel a lump forming in my throat and my eyes started to prickle.

Rachel nodded at me, encouraging me to carry on. 'I was yelling at her to wait for me, but she couldn't hear 'cos the cars were too loud. I couldn't cross the road to get to her as there were too many cars. I kept trying, but they all swerved to avoid me, so I had to keep jumping back.' I stopped for breath. It was coming back thick and fast now, and I didn't like how it was making me feel.

I took a deep breath and closed my eyes, seeing in my head the end of my dream. With a shaky voice, I told Rachel that she had disappeared over the hill without looking back and I'd been stuck there on my own by a motorway. When Rachel asked me how it made me feel, I burst into tears. Rachel handed me a tissue, but didn't ask any questions. I cried for a bit, and then I realized I wasn't sad, I was angry: Ellie had never said goodbye.

TWENTY

It was an ordinary miserable day in the Hunter household when our lives were turned the right way up again almost as fast as they'd been turned upside down. Mum and Dad had dragged me and Lee to see Mum's great aunt Nina, who was dying in hospital. I had no idea why we all had to go, but suspected it was so we'd be remembered in her will. It was really depressing 'cos she was slipping in and out of consciousness, and didn't have a clue who any of us were. It made me want to make the most of my life.

I was hoping we'd get back in time for me to go round to Brian's for band practice, but Dad wouldn't drop me off. I was gutted. It was hard enough to get any time to be with Brian as it was, without Dad sticking his nose in. I was worried he might twig that no one else at school liked me much. What if he decided he didn't want to be with me any more?

I went straight upstairs to have a bath. Just my luck, I thought to myself. The door was locked and I could hear someone in the shower. Thinking it was Dan, I went into my room to wait; he never took that long. A few minutes later the door slammed and I could hear

Dan's voice. 'So who was in the shower then?' I thought as I went downstairs.

I opened my mouth to ask, but when I walked into the room and saw my family assembled before me with sombre faces, suddenly it didn't feel so important. Dan looked pale and serious as he stood before Mum and Dad. Lee had been stuffing his face, but the atmosphere in the lounge seemed to have robbed him of his appetite.

'I've got something to tell you,' said Dan to Mum and Dad. Then he looked at me and Lee. My stomach tightened and I got goose bumps. I didn't like the look of this at all.

'What is it?' asked Dad in his most stoic voice. But Dan looked away. He didn't seem able to find the words. I started to feel sick. Whatever this was about, it was serious and the only thing I could think of that would affect all of us was Ellie. I braced myself for the worst, but Dan couldn't even look at us, let alone tell us our sister was dead. I glanced at Lee, who looked terrified. He was obviously thinking the same.

'Come on Dan, what is it?' asked Mum through trembling lips. 'You're scaring me.' Dad went to sit next to her and put his arm around her protectively. Dan looked pained and the silence seemed to last an eternity. He was just about to say it, when we heard the bathroom door open and someone come down the stairs. Dan looked at the door nervously and we all watched it open with baited breath.

'The thing is …' he started awkwardly. And then the most amazing thing happened, the thing none of us thought we'd ever see. Ellie walked in. She wasn't dead; she was alive and she was there, standing right in front of us in a towel and dripping water on the carpet. We all stared at her in amazement, our mouths hanging open. Was this real? Was Ellie back for good?

* * *

It was weird at first. What do you say to the sister you haven't seen for almost two years and who you thought was dead? Mum grabbed her and hugged her for what seemed like forever, and then she started crying. Then Ellie started crying, and then we all did, even Dad, and piled in and had a massive hug.

She didn't say much, other than that she hadn't been kidnapped or held against her will. I think she was overwhelmed by us all being in her face suddenly and said she didn't want to talk about where she'd been. I didn't want to let her out of my sight and refused to admit I was tired, but Ellie got up first and went to bed, only after promising she'd talk more in the morning.

I couldn't sleep at all that night. There was too much going on in my head. I had never wanted to believe she was dead and had always tried to keep my hope alive, but I never imagined the outcome would be as happy as this one. I didn't think I deserved it.

When it got to four o'clock, I knew there wasn't much point in trying to get to sleep. I got up and stole into Ellie's room. I hadn't been in there for months; I'd found it too upsetting. I couldn't believe she was back. She was really there, her breathing causing her old familiar duvet to rise and fall. I looked at her, making sure she was real, but looking wasn't enough and I gently touched her arm.

It must have only felt like a whisper, but she woke with a start, cold anger flashing across her face, but then she seemed to remember who I was and where she was, and she smiled. I hadn't seen that smile in ages and it made me cry. Without saying a word, she shifted over in her bed and lifted up the duvet in an invitation to join her. I did, climbing in eagerly, snuggling up to my big sis and sleeping like a baby.

Heaven never lasts long in our house and it came crashing down around us the next day when Dad found out that Dan had known Ellie was back almost a week before we did. He said it took him ages to work out how he was going to tell us, but Dad had thought there was something suss going on that he should know about. Personally, I didn't see what all the fuss was about. She was back. Couldn't we just be happy?

The row woke Ellie up and she came downstairs in her nightie. She looked worried and scared. Dan and Dad had never yelled at each other like this before she went away. But then, a lot of things had changed since she went away.

Dan seemed tense right from the word go. I wasn't sure if he did know more than he was letting on, or if the old resentment was starting to creep back in. He and Ellie always had an odd relationship. She always knew exactly what buttons to press to wind him up. He was the first to stop looking at her through rose-coloured specs and actually feel annoyed with her for what she had put us all through.

Looking back, he was probably right. She didn't seem to be showing a whole lot of remorse, but at the time, none of the rest of us wanted to admit it. We were all scared that if we pushed her too far, then she'd go off again. It was like she was holding the whole family to ransom.

I can always tell when Dan's going to blow. He doesn't drink loads like Dad, or disappear like Lee, he goes quiet for a while, and then takes his rally car out. It used to scare the life out of me. I knew how fast he drove it when I was an unlucky passenger, so it made me feel sick to think of the speed he'd do on his own.

One night, he was tetchy with Ellie over dinner and she was probing him about what she was supposed to have done to annoy him. He started reeling off a list of the ways she'd made our lives a misery, the money we'd spent looking for her and all that stuff, when Dad grabbed him and warned him to shut it or get out. Ellie made it worse by grinning at him.

Ordinarily, it would have been at that point that he'd have reached for his keys, but the car was off the road 'cos he and Dad had been welding the sump or something. I could see him struggling to keep it all in, but then he just let rip at her, calling her every name under the sun and telling her how selfish she was.

'Mum's a wreck, Dad's an alcoholic, Lee's going off the rails and did you happen to know your kid sister's got an unhealthy appetite for cutting her arms up?' he yelled at her, bits of his food flying out of his mouth. It was too much for Ellie to take in. I could have killed Dan for including me. I felt ashamed and embarrassed. I didn't want Ellie to know I'd been a wreck without her. I ran upstairs and flung myself crying onto my bed. How could I have been so stupid as to think Ellie being back would make everything better?

* * *

Things got quieter in the house after that. Dan had a massive hypo 'cos of his diabetes and ended up in hospital. It happens sometimes when he's really stressed out. Mum spent a lot of time visiting and Dad buried his head under a car bonnet as usual, but at least the house was empty so I could have Brian round whenever I wanted.

A few days later, I'd done my homework and was lying on my bed trying to think of dreams I'd had in the past week. I usually remembered them when I woke up 'cos they still seemed so vivid, but I found myself wondering what happens to your dreams during the day. Where do they go? It scared me that you could never get them back once they'd gone.

Brian called round with a CD he'd been meaning to lend me for weeks. I knew it was just a pretext to see if I was okay, but I didn't mind. It was nice to have him all to myself for once and not have to pretend. He'd also been gagging to meet Ellie ever since I told him she was back, so I put him out of his misery and introduced them. I soon wished I hadn't, as he was bowled over by her. Ellie's really gorgeous anyway, but she's got this confidence thing going on that I haven't and it makes her irresistible to men.

Unfortunately for me, Ellie told me before she went out clubbing that she hadn't been so taken with him. She said his whole look was scruffy and I could do better. I was gutted; I'd been desperate for her to like him. Ellie's opinion meant so much to me. I'd always looked up to her and taken her advice about everything. Falling for Brian had seemed so natural, but now I found myself questioning our whole relationship.

'Hey, what's up?' he asked, grinning and nudging me.

'Nothing,' I replied. I'd been lost in a world of my own and I couldn't tell him I was wondering whether we really should be together. He leaned over and kissed me. My heart flipped as it always did and I pulled him closer to me. I'd had to make loads of choices without Ellie's approval while she'd been away. Maybe she was wrong about this, I knew what I wanted and that was Brian. The thing was, we were starting to want each other A LOT.

We lay back on the bed without breaking away from the kiss. It felt wonderful, deep and hot and intense. Brian pulled my school blouse out of my waistband, and my skin tingled when he slipped his hand under my bra and cupped my boob. I gripped him tighter. He was getting harder and harder to resist. We heard a noise somewhere out on the street and stopped, panting, ears pricked up, hoping we weren't about to be disturbed. When we were satisfied the coast was clear, I initiated another long, hard kiss.

After a while, Brian broke it off and fumbled with the tiny buttons on my shirt. I felt excited. This was the furthest we'd gone and I liked it. He put his hands on my shoulders and started to push my shirt off, reaching around the back of me to undo my bra. Just as I was pulling my arm out of the sleeve, it snagged and I felt as if I'd been stung.

'What's the matter?' whispered Brian nuzzling me. He'd sensed that I'd frozen. I pulled my blouse tight around me and moved away from him, suddenly wishing he'd stop. I just wanted him to go away and leave me alone.

'You liked it the other day.' He tried, but failed to pull me back over to him. He was right, but a few days ago I didn't have a brand new gash across my arm, thanks to Ellie and Dan's row. It was like he read the guilt scrawled across my face and instinctively knew why I didn't want to take my blouse off.

'You're cutting again, aren't you?' he said, his face hard and cold. I didn't say anything, but I suppose my silence confirmed his fears. He silently buttoned himself up and left without saying a word.

TWENTY-ONE

I didn't sleep at all that night and pretended I was ill when Mum tried to get me up for school the next day. Brian had been the only thing keeping me going and now we were over I just couldn't face it. After everyone else had left for school or work, Ellie came into my room with a tray. She'd made me porridge with treacle like she used to when I was ill as a kid. I was glad it was just going to be me and her for the day.

We took my duvet downstairs and snuggled up as we watched some chat shows. I told Ellie that Brian and I had split up. I didn't tell her why. She's not easy to keep secrets from, though. She just knows when you're doing it. I suppose I was stupid to think she wouldn't try to talk to me about what Dan told her.

'Do you really cut yourself?' she asked me. I felt put on the spot. I loved Ellie to bits, but I really didn't want to talk about this, not with her, not with anyone. I offered to make us some drinks, but she grabbed me and made me sit back down. 'Do you?' Eventually I nodded. She looked really sad and I felt guilty for worrying her.

'Why?' Her voice was gentle and concerned, not shrill and hysterical like Mum's. I shrugged. It's not like I hadn't asked myself the same question a million times. 'Is it school? Are you stressed about your exams?' I frowned and shook my head. They were the last things on my mind. 'Is it a confidence thing?' she asked. 'Don't you like yourself?'

'Not really.' I couldn't think of when I ever did, though, and I hadn't always felt this need to cut.

She stroked a strand of hair away from my face and tucked it behind my ear. 'You do know you're gorgeous, don't you?' she asked. She looked serious, but I think she was just being nice 'cos I was having such a tough time. I looked away from her, embarrassed. 'You used to talk to me about everything,' she said. I'd missed our chats, but she was the one who disappeared without letting us know she was even alive. 'Please talk to me.' She looked so plaintive.

'I don't know why,' I mumbled. 'It just makes me feel better.'

'But why do you feel bad in the first place?' she asked. I shrugged again and said, 'I don't find it that easy to talk to people about feelings and stuff. I don't want to be a burden to anyone. I'd rather just deal with it myself.' She rolled the sleeve of my PJs up and looked at my arm, curdled with old and new scars. She stroked one gently with her thumb. I flinched, but didn't pull away.

'Doing this to yourself isn't dealing with it,' she said, and I knew she was right. She knew not to push it any further and just gave me a cuddle for a while. It was so good to have her back again. I couldn't believe I'd managed so long without her.

I went upstairs to have a shower while she made us something naughty for lunch. Ellie's a great cook. She had a lot of practice making meals for us lot when Mum and Dad were both working late. When I came back downstairs, lunch was ready and there was a pile of printouts from the Internet on the table. As we ate, she explained that she'd found out I wasn't the only one who cut myself. There were literally thousands of people who did it, and there was a name for it – self-harm.

***

Ellie was giving me a make-over when Lee got home from school. He said people were asking where I was, but I found it hard to believe anyone had even noticed. When I tried to get out of him which people in particular, he went all vague. He does that when he first gets home from school. He's fine once he's eaten. When I tried later, he told me Brian had been pretty worried about me. I scoffed at him. Yeah, right.

Later on, I was lying on Ellie's bed, chatting to her as she got ready to go out, when the doorbell went. I ran downstairs, thinking it would be her date, and was astonished to see Brian standing on the doorstep. I didn't know what to do or what to say. It was weird to think he wasn't my boyfriend anymore. I hadn't realized how sad I was until I saw him.

'What's all this about us splitting up?' he asked, stepping inside before giving me a chance to invite him.

'Ssh!' I didn't want the whole world to know.

'Oh, it's you,' said Ellie with disdain from the top of the stairs. Brian ignored her and she went back into her room to dry her hair.

'I never said we were over,' he hissed at me.

'Well, you didn't exactly give me the impression you wanted to be with me,' I hissed back hotly, annoyed he assumed the decision to split would have been his anyway. The doorbell rang again and this time it was Ellie's date. I dragged Brian by the sleeve up to my room. We needed peace and privacy to talk. I shut the door behind us.

'So is that it, then?' demanded Brian. 'I have to find out from your brother I'm dumped, 'cos you can't even be bothered to tell me yourself?'

'I didn't dump you; you dumped me.'

'I didn't!' But you told me you'd stopped all that. I thought I was helping you get better.'

'You are,' I said, stepping closer to him.

'I can't be doing a very good job,' he said dismally.

'It's more complicated than that,' I told him. 'But it's honestly nothing to do with you. I'm really happy with you, Brian.' He didn't look very comforted. 'I love you.' He looked shocked. I was, too. I hadn't meant to say it. I didn't even realize I did until that moment. I smiled at him to confirm I meant it. He smiled right back.

We went over to the bed and lay with our arms around each other, kissing and talking. Sometimes we just looked at each other, as if we were having a conversation without words. Brian spoke after a while. He still had stuff on his mind and I had to work really hard to reassure him.

'I understand you do it when you feel annoyed, like everything's getting on top of you. But if you just want to let it all out, then take it out on me.' I laughed. I didn't think he was serious until he looked hurt.

'I'm serious. Hit me, punch me … kick me if you like. I can take it. Just stop doing it to yourself. Please. For me.' I felt awful. I'd had no idea this was affecting him so much. I pulled him closer to me and kissed the top of his head, determined to put an end to my self-harm. I realized it wasn't just me who was getting cut up by it.

* * *

When Dan came out of hospital a few days later, we all made a special effort to pussy-foot around him. Even Ellie forgot how much he wound her up and made him loads of nice food. Nothing seemed to lift his spirits. He hated being diabetic and feeling different from all his mates. He was meant to have bed-rest for at least a week, but there was no way he was going to play the part of an invalid any more than was necessary.

The row started when Ellie caught him out of bed. She chided him gently and she tried to push him back to the bedroom, but Dan grabbed her and told her not to push him around. She flared up back at him and they had the most almighty scrap. I was terrified: I wasn't strong enough to come between them and Lee didn't want to get involved. Luckily, Mum came home and put an end to it, but not before yelling at them both. She was particularly mad at Ellie 'cos Dan was still really ill.

If there's one thing Ellie hates, it's being treated like a kid. She started yelling at Mum and told her she wished she'd never come home. I couldn't believe things had got so serious all of a sudden. She ran upstairs and I saw her through a crack in the door, ramming random belongings into her holdall. My throat went dry. She wasn't seriously leaving, was she? She flung her door open and saw me standing there. She kissed my cheek, then dragged her bag downstairs.

'This time I won't be back,' she yelled at Mum as she opened the front door and disappeared into the night. The whole house was still for a moment. I couldn't believe no one was going after her. I ran down the stairs and into the street.

'Ellie!' I screamed. 'Don't go. Please don't go.' At first she didn't turn around. Then she stopped. I ran to catch up with her. She was crying, too.

'Go back inside,' she said. I shook my head. 'Do it, Lisa, or you won't see me again,' she said, forcing her voice to sound cold.

'But where are you going? What are you going to do?' I wailed.

'I'll be at a mate's. I'll call you when I get settled.' And with that, she wrestled herself free from my grip, leaving me sobbing in the street.

TWENTY-TWO

I didn't hear from Ellie the next day, or the one after. By the third day, I was desperate. Even though I'd promised myself not to, the temptation to cut was too great. I couldn't keep all that agony inside me. If I had, I would have exploded.

I suppose I'd got slack about making sure no one was in the house when I was doing it. I thought I had my hearing so highly trained that I would know if someone was within a mile of coming into my room. How wrong was I? I was feeling a lot calmer and was enjoying the red when Dad burst into the room and caught me. There was no way I could pretend anything else was going on. I still had the stained and splayed scissors in my hand.

'What the hell are you doing?' he growled. And there was me thinking I'd been really clever by cutting on my legs. I thought if people saw my arms were healing they'd get off my case. I thought they'd think I'd stopped and I would be able to carry on in private, and it would remain the secret I had always intended it to be.

'Sort yourself out and get yourself downstairs now.' When Dad spoke to me like that, it was hard to think that he felt anything other than hate for me. I took my special box into the bathroom and cleaned myself up. I deliberately took ages dabbing wet cotton wool onto the slits in my skin. I was painstaking in my administration of Savlon and made a meal out of cutting the plaster to the exact sizes I needed.

I pressed my ear against the locked door before coming out. I wanted to make sure the coast was clear. I could hear Mum and Dad yelling downstairs and felt terrible that I'd been a lit match in the box of fireworks that was their marriage. I could hear Dad going on about me being a crackpot and saying that this was how nutters behaved. Mum was trying to defend me, but she didn't do a very good job. How could she when she didn't have a clue what was going on in my head?

Then it all went a bit quiet. I crept out onto the landing, wondering why the shouting had stopped, and then I heard my dad speaking on the phone. My heart sank when I realized he was having a go at Rachel.

'Don't you Mister Hunter me!' he yelled. 'Just 'cos you've got letters after your name, it doesn't give you the authority to patronize me.' It went quiet again for a few moments.

'Please, Les, this isn't the way,' I heard Mum whisper, urging him to put the phone down.

'No, you listen!' His voice was even louder. 'You won't be seeing my daughter for any other sessions, 'cos I'm putting a stop to them. She doesn't need you filling her head with any more mumbo-jumbo claptrap.' And with that, he slammed the phone down. I was sitting on the top stair. I felt mortified. Rachel had been so nice to me and I didn't want to stop seeing her.

Just then, the living room door flung open and Dad came storming out. He had turned puce and it frightened me. I thought he was going to come upstairs to have a go at me, but he didn't. Instead, he barged out of the front door and went into the garage. Mum stood in the hallway, as bemused as I was. I don't think she knew I was there.

A few moments later, Dad came back into the house, his toolbox in his hand. I was scared he'd lost it. What was he going to do? Hammer my hands to the table so I couldn't do it any more? I backed away from him and went to lock myself in my room. I didn't like the look of this one bit.

'What are you doing now?' asked Mum, exasperated.

'If a shrink can't sort her out, then I can,' he said. 'She won't be able to do it if there's no door on her room,' he said, heading up the stairs.

'You can't do that, what about her privacy?'

'She's forfeited her right to privacy by keeping doing it,' he said, the toolbox clanking on the floor outside my room. I could hear him rummaging for a screwdriver.

* * *

I was already miserable when I went to school the next day, but I felt even worse when I was confronted by Brian talking to Zara. They hadn't spoken in months. She hated him for dumping her for me. So what was going on?

The thought of them seeing each other behind my back hit me and my heart skipped a beat. I was trembling as I walked over. They seemed to stop talking when they saw me coming. Brian grinned at me and stretched his arm out, inviting me to hold his hand. I did so tentatively. He certainly wasn't behaving like he had a guilty conscience. Was I just being paranoid?

'What were you talking to her about?' I asked, as casually as I could, as we headed for our first lesson. We'd got to the stage in all our subjects where we were recapping what we'd learned before our exams started.

'She's had a tough time with Adam, you know.' That wasn't the reassurance I needed that he still loved me. I did know Zara had been through it. Her brother was going to be in a wheelchair for life and there was a massive court case coming up over the summer 'cos her sister had accused a footballer of raping her. I can't remember his name, but no one believed he did it and all the boys had started taking it out on Zara.

'She was asking me what I was going to get you for your birthday,' he said, with a twinkle in his eye.

'I'm surprised she even remembers when it is.'

'Listen, I know she's been a real bitch in the past, but I think all this stuff has made her grow up a bit.' I didn't answer, but must have looked dubious.

'Honestly, she's a different person.'

Brian's got a habit of seeing the good in everybody, but it worried me the way he was singing her praises. I got the chance to test the water for myself later on. We were getting changed for netball when Abby went to the loo. Mrs Mitchell came in and blew her whistle at us all and told us to hurry up. Everyone else filed out and just as Zara was leaving she raised her eyes at me. I knew she was as fed up with Mrs Mitchell as we all were. My instinct told me to ignore her – she'd hardly wanted to be my mate when I was having a bad time – but I didn't. I smiled and she smiled back.

I was goalkeeper and she was wing defence. All the action was happening at the other end of the pitch.

'How's it all going?' she asked me casually.

'All right,' I replied, trying to mirror her nonchalance,

even though my heart was racing. I couldn't believe I was having a civilized conversation with my tormentor after all this time.

'Listen,' she said, a sincere look on her face, 'I'm so sorry about all the things I said and did to you. I was a bitch.' I was stunned. She really had changed. The Zara I knew would never have admitted to being wrong in a million years.

'Forget it,' I said. As long as I knew she wasn't going to give me any more grief, I wasn't going to bear a grudge.

* * *

I was nervous as I walked to school on the morning of my first exam. I was trying to memorize my King Lear quotations when someone grabbed me from behind. I jumped out of my skin. When I turned round, I was thrilled to see it was Ellie. I hugged her.

'Where have you been?' I said, all Shakespeare fleeing my mind.

'You know, here and there.' Ellie likes being elusive. 'How's the land lying at home?' she asked. 'Safe for me to come back yet?'

'Dad caught me cutting. He's taken my bedroom door off.'

'Oh, what? That's not going to help you get better, is it?' I shook my head. I agreed with her, but there was no standing up to Dad. 'Listen, this is for you.' She handed me a little green Good Luck teddy. 'I know you'll ace it. You're a brain-box, unlike me.' I grinned at her; I was feeling pretty confident. 'You go and do your exam, and we'll deal with it later.'

As it turned out, Ellie didn't have to do anything. When Lee and I got home from school, Mum and Dad had gone.

Aunt Nina had died in the night and they were on their way up to Newcastle to help clear the house and arrange the funeral. They were going to be gone a few days.

Ellie got Lee to help her put the door back on and then she took me out shopping for a dress to wear to the end of term prom. When we got back, the four of us ordered pizzas and watched some videos. It was nice without Mum and Dad yelling at us or each other and I really felt hope for the future, like everything was going to be okay.

TWENTY-THREE

I was so excited about the prom I could hardly sleep. Brian was picking me up at seven. Ellie was going to do my make-up and she'd told me Brian could stay the night if I wanted, as long as I didn't tell Dan. At first I was shocked, but then she told me that she was my age when she lost it and she could see how much Brian meant to me.

It got me thinking about whether I really should go for it with him that night. We'd almost done it a few times, but now there was a real possibility it could happen I suddenly felt scared. Brian had done it before. He knew what to do. I had an idea, but what if I made a fool of myself? What if I did something wrong?

I spent all day cleaning and tidying my room. I took all my teddies off the bed and changed the sheets. I was going for a more seductive look. I went into town to buy make-up in Boots, and while Ellie was choosing me a lip-gloss, I sneaked off to the homes section and bought some candles. I made sure I had the perfect CD ready in the player and, of course, the condoms we'd been given at school all those months ago in the drawer of my bedside table.

Just as I was having a panic about them being out of date, there was a knock on my bedroom door. I instinctively sat on the condoms and Lee came in. He always looked glum, but this time he looked *really* glum. I wondered if Mum and Dad had called to say they were coming back early. It would be just their style to ruin all our fun.

'Has Abby said anything about me recently?' he asked, trying to sound casual. They'd split up a few weeks ago, though he wouldn't tell me why. I wasn't exactly bosom buddies with Abby, but we chatted about stuff and she did tell me that he hadn't been honest with her. One girl finding him attractive was strange, but the thought of him cheating on her with someone else baffled me.

'Not really,' I lied. She'd made me promise not to tell him she missed him like crazy.

'Oh.' He looked disappointed. 'So there's no point me asking her to the prom then?' I didn't know what I should do. She would have been chuffed a week ago. I know she was hoping he would ask, but that day? The prom was only four hours away and she'd already agreed to go with Noel.

I told him to do what he thought was best. I was too distracted with my own preparations to worry about his problems. I still had to shave my legs and file my nails, and wash my hair – oh, and choose my underwear. Lee went off with Norman and Bombhead, and I told him I'd see him there.

Ellie gave me a facial, manicure, pedicure, hair treatment and wax. I felt like a star when I slipped my newly moisturized self into my brand new dress. I wasn't quite ready when Brian arrived, but that was how it was meant to be – I'd seen it in films. He looked lovely in his tuxedo and he gave me a rose. Ellie swooned and Dan pretended to throw up. I think they were secretly pleased I was going to have such a great night.

***

When we got to school, the gym was decorated and the disco was already going, even though no one was dancing yet. We bumped into the rest of the band and their dates by the fruit punch and it felt great to be part of the gang. Zara and Abby were really nice to me and said they thought Brian and me might be prom king and queen. I wrinkled my nose at them, even though it had been my secret fantasy for weeks.

We had some food and listened to the teachers make speeches about what a great year we'd been. Brian reckoned that they said the same thing every year and we shouldn't let our heads get too big. A few prizes were handed out and a formal announcement about what to do in case of a fire and then finally the night was ours. The lights went low and the teachers made themselves scarce as Brian led me to the dance floor.

'You look amazing,' he whispered in my ear. I kissed his cheek as a thank you. I pulled my face away from his so I could look at him, my Brian. He was gorgeous as ever.

'Ellie says you can stay at ours tonight,' I whispered back. He looked at me intently, not daring to believe the implications of what I was saying. 'In my room with me …' I added carefully. What if he didn't want to? What if he thought I was cheap for asking?

'You sure?' His voice was soft and serious. I smiled and nodded. I'd never been more sure of anything in my life.

He smiled too, and held me close. I never wanted that moment to end. Everything was perfect.

Suddenly, someone tapped on the microphone. It was Mr Berrington, the headmaster. My heart flipped when I saw a small table next to him with the prom king and queen's crowns on it.

'And now it's time to announce this year's king and queen,' he said, sounding like a bingo caller. He lowered his glasses on his nose and read from a piece of paper. The whole world stood still and I was too scared even to breathe, but then it came, the moment I thought I'd never see: Mr Berrington called out our names.

We were both grinning when we went on stage to be crowned. Everyone else was whooping and clapping, and whistling. We stayed up on the stage and were joined by the rest of the band. We had five minutes to set up before the disco stopped for half an hour for our set. We'd been practising hard and our performance was really tight. I knew we were going to blow everyone away.

I felt a buzz of adrenalin surge through my body when Brian struck the first chord. A few weeks ago, singing in front of the whole school would have been my worst nightmare. We'd managed to persuade Mr Berrington to let us use the overhead projector. We thought it would be really cool to flash images from the yearbook Steph had put together up on a screen behind us as we played.

The first song went without a hitch and we were all gaining confidence. I was looking forward to singing the song I'd written for Brian. Somehow it meant so much more that night and I didn't care if the other kids worked out it was about him. I wanted everyone to know how much I loved him.

Just as we were building up to the second chorus, I noticed people slowly stopping dancing and looking up at us on the stage. They were pointing at the screen behind us and laughing, but it wasn't a funny ha-ha kind of laugh. It was like a mist of unease spread across the hall.

I thought one of the slides must have gone in the machine upside down, but then why this weird reaction? It felt like the whole world was looking at me and Brian and I couldn't work out why. Then, at the back of the hall, Zara started yelling at someone.

'You bitch!' she screamed, as she lunged at Steph, who had been working the projector. I wondered what was going on. I turned around. It felt everything was moving in slow motion and the sounds in the hall distorted in my ears as if I was under water. I looked at the screen behind me, and my mouth fell open in shock. I felt like I'd been slapped. There, six-foot tall, for the whole world to see, was Brian snogging Zara.

I looked at him for an explanation. He too was staring, shocked. Maybe it was an old photo, I tried to rationalize to myself. But his eyes said it all. They were brimming with guilt. I couldn't hear him speak, even though the hall had fallen silent, but I made out him mouthing sorry at me. My whole world came crashing around my ears and the last thing I remember was running, as if for my life, out of the hall.

* * *

I didn't know how I'd got home, or how long I'd been there, but I was woken up by Ellie banging on the bathroom door. I lifted my tear-stained cheek from the cold floor tiles and tried to sit up, but pain shot through my arm and I remembered the deepest cut. Globules of blood had jellified around the gash itself, but it still looked wet and there was a darkening pool slowly growing on the floor where I had been lying.

'Lisa, are you in there?' came Ellie's voice again. I couldn't have spoken if I'd wanted to. I felt like someone had poured a bucket of sand down my throat. I heard her walk away and go into my room. 'Oh my God!' I heard her say. My mind was fuzzy. It hurt when I tried to remember what would make her react like that. What blood was left in my body ran cold as I realized I had left all my cutting gear on the floor. I hadn't even had a chance to clean the stain from the carpet.

I heard her leg it down the stairs and pick up the phone. I started to shake. I was weak and cold, but I had to stop her. I really didn't want Mum and Dad to know about this. My legs were shaky as I used the side of the bath to haul myself up. My feet hurt and I groaned with the pain of the blisters and also the memory of losing Ellie's shoes.

I was unsteady as I reached for the door. My legs buckled beneath me like a newborn foal's. I think I must have blacked out again as the next thing I heard was a louder, more anxious rapping on the door, and Dan's voice.

'Lisa, it's Dan. Please open the door.'

'We want to help you,' added Ellie plaintively. It sounded like she was crying. The sound seemed to open the floodgates. I could feel a tide rushing through every part of me. I gasped when it hit my throat and before I knew it, I was sobbing. I reached a shaky, blood-streaked hand up to the door and unlocked it. Suddenly Dan and Ellie were in. They both looked horrified. Dan scooped me up in his arms and ran with me to his car.

TWENTY-FOUR

I'd never been to hospital before, apart from when I was born I suppose, but I couldn't remember that. For the first time in my life, I was too out of it to be frightened by Dan's driving. Ellie was in the back seat with me. She'd put a towel around my throbbing arm and I was lying with my head on her lap, the loss of blood and sudden motion making me feel disorientated and sick.

I felt worse when we got there. My head was lolling like a rag doll as Dan carried me into Casualty. The smell hit me first, clean and heavy in my nostrils. Ellie ran over to reception. It was only under the harsh bright lights that I realized how pale and small and scared she looked. She had to fill in a form and then we were directed to a load of seats where other sick and injured people were waiting.

At first, none of us spoke. I sat between them with my head on Dan's shoulder. He had his arm around me and Ellie was holding my good hand. I felt scared and wondered if I was going to die. I looked down and saw that my dress was ruined. How had things got this bad? The memory of Zara and Brian seeped back into my head like yellow poison. I tried to tell Ellie about what had happened, but all I could do was cry. I couldn't even do that properly; it felt like I'd run out of tears hours ago.

After three hours of waiting, Dan was ready to go through the roof. He'd been checking my arm and it still looked pretty bad. The towel was almost sodden by that stage. Ellie tried to get him to calm down for my sake, but he felt helpless. It was the dead of night and other patients were getting tetchy, too. Some of them had been waiting for longer than we had.

Just when I was scared Dan was going to punch someone, a nurse came over to try to calm him down. She looked at the form we'd filled in and asked our relation to each other. I let Dan and Ellie do all the talking. Then she gently lifted the lip of the towel and peeked underneath. She took a deep breath and frowned.

'How did this happen?' she asked gently. I didn't know what to say and I didn't have the energy to speak. I didn't want to tell her the truth anyway; I was too ashamed.

'It was an accident,' said Dan defensively.

'She does it to herself,' added Ellie. 'She just did it too deep.' Dan shot her a look. We both wished she hadn't said it. 'She needs help,' she added firmly in response. 'This is too big for just us to deal with.'

The nurse seemed to look at me with different eyes after that. She wasn't so warm and gentle as she'd first appeared. 'Would you like to follow me?' she said to us all, even though she'd already started walking. We hurried after her, Dan and Ellie supporting me. We went into a cubicle and I was told to sit on the bed. It was high and Dan had to lift me up. Then he went and waited outside.

The nurse laid out all the equipment she needed next to me and started cleaning me up. She was quick and thorough, but didn't try to put me at ease.

'You'd be surprised how many girls cut themselves,' she said to Ellie grimly, as if I wasn't there. Ellie smiled. She was hopeful she might get some advice. 'I bet this won't be the last time we see her. It never is.'

I felt like I'd been told I had a terminal illness. I looked at Ellie. She knew I was about to cry. She came over to the bed and stroked my hair, hushing away the tears.

'Is there anything we can do to help her?' asked Ellie.

'Yes,' said the nurse, tapping the side of my head. 'Find out what's going on up here and maybe she'll realize it's not doing anyone any good.'

'She's been having counselling,' said Ellie. She didn't want the nurse to think we hadn't been trying to sort it out.

'Well, she needs more,' said the nurse quite sternly. 'There are better ways to cope than this.' She tied a knot in the last stitch. 'There are people out there with serious injuries; there are people dying,' she said, looking at me for the first time. 'Have a read of this,' she added, handing me a leaflet. She smiled, but I don't think she meant it, and Ellie and I were left alone.

'Stupid old bag,' said Ellie, helping me down. I agreed. Even though the nurse had stitched my arm up and given me a shot for the pain, somehow she'd made me feel a whole lot worse.

* * *

When we got home, the sight of Lee looking frantic made us realize we'd forgotten to let him know where we'd been. He was shocked at the sight of me and knew instantly what I'd done. He had no idea about what had gone on at the prom and I realized that I hadn't actually seen him there, or any of his mates for that matter.

He had a million questions for me. They all did. But I had no answers. I was a physical and emotional wreck and all I needed was to go to bed. I dragged my heavy body up the stairs. Ellie came after me to see if I wanted a bath, but the noise of all those thoughts jostling around in my head was too much. I just needed to be on my own, in bed.

Hours later, I woke up, my head thick and pounding. I turned over to look at the time on my alarm clock, and saw the candles and condoms I'd had ready for my night with Brian. Lee knocked gently on the door. He'd brought me the portable T.V. from Mum and Dad's room. He seemed awkward.

'I'm sorry I wasn't there for you,' he said. I didn't want him feeling guilty. I didn't need a bodyguard. Then Ellie came in with a cup of tea, followed by Dan with a bag of doughnuts. They all sat on my bed with me and we tried to talk. I felt so bad for freaking them all out like that, but I'd freaked myself out, too.

I told them what had happened with Brian and Zara, and even though they couldn't get their heads around what I'd done, they did seem to understand it a bit more. I told them I'd scared myself, which was good, as I really had no intention of doing it again, ever. Although I was physically weak, somehow I felt stronger, like something cathartic had happened to me.

When the atmosphere at home got a bit too sombre, I went out for a walk. I had a lot of stuff in my head that needed sorting out and the one person I knew who could help me with that was Rachel. It was Saturday, so I was half expecting her not to be there, but I was so relieved when she was. She told me Dad didn't want her to see me any more, but she must have seen how desperate I was to talk.

I told her about everything that had happened, about deciding to sleep with Brian, being made prom queen and then finding out he'd been cheating on me. I showed her the blood-black stitches on my arm, and she looked sad for me and said it must really hurt. I told her it did, but I wasn't talking about my arm; I was talking about how I felt inside.

'I feel like such a freak,' I told her.

'Hey, you're not a freak.' she assured me. 'I'm not sure how anyone would cope with finding out their boyfriend was cheating like that in front of the whole school.' I nodded. Thinking about it, I knew she was right.

'Do you want to stop hurting yourself or do you like it?' she asked. I'd never dared admit to anyone before that I needed it, that it was like an addiction.

'I don't want to hurt my family any more,' I admitted. 'I want to find another way.' She seemed pleased with me and told me I'd made loads of progress. She taught me this exercise that is almost like counting to ten before you shout at someone you're angry with. If I could just delay the impulse to do it a little longer each time, then maybe, just maybe one day I'd be able to stop.

Rachel warned me it would be a long, hard slog, but she'd helped loads of people before me to control this thing that they'd always thought was in control of them. I knew I could do it. It was like all the anger I felt for Brian was converting into power, power to be able to be on my own and not be afraid.

I hated him and loved him and missed him all at the same time, but Rachel made me see that maybe what had happened had happened for a reason, and that he'd actually done me a favour. When I thought about it, our relationship hadn't been that equal. I'd obviously loved and adored him far more than he did me, but then I hid behind him, too. I was happy to be in his shadow, 'cos in the shadows is where the scared and frightened Lisa, who needed to hurt herself, lived.

TWENTY-FIVE

Mum and Dad got home from the funeral the next day, which was also my birthday. I was sixteen and hoped against hope that this would be a new beginning for me. Ellie, Dan, Lee and I had all agreed that we wouldn't tell Mum and Dad what had happened. We'd talked about it a lot and realized we actually coped pretty well as a foursome.

I tried to act as normally as I could, even though my cut was still hurting and it was starting to get itchy. Ellie cooked a big roast and we were just sitting down to eat when the doorbell went. Lee went to answer it. We all assumed it was one of his mates as he didn't come back straight away. Then we heard shouting and went into the hall to investigate.

'You stay away from her, do you hear me?' Lee was pushing Brian out of the door. When he saw me, he looked more hopeful.

'Lisa, I can explain.' I thought I'd been coping pretty well with not having him around, but the sight of him tugged at my heart. I wanted to hate him, but I didn't.

'What's going on?' bellowed Dad. He always got more grouchy than usual when he was hungry.

'Nothing,' said Dan, glaring at Brian.

'I want to talk to Lisa,' said Brian, speaking directly to Dad.

'Well, come on in then,' said Mum, oblivious to any of the undercurrents. 'There's plenty to go round.'

'Actually, we might just go for a quick walk,' I said, grabbing my jacket from the banister, conscious of six pairs of eyes flicking on to me.

'But it's your birthday dinner,' said Ellie frostily. 'He can wait.' I didn't bother to answer; I just shut the door behind us. It was weird, me and Brian being alone. Everything had shifted and there was this huge chasm between us. I didn't really have much to say to him, but I was morbidly interested in his excuse.

'Everyone at school knows you went to hospital,' he told me. I supposed I was stupid to think they'd never find out. 'I'm sorry,' he said, when we got to the end of the road. He was looking me right in the eyes and I knew he meant it, but he'd meant it when he said it to Zara after cheating on her with Steph. It didn't change what he'd done.

Ironically we ended up in the graveyard where we'd had our first kiss. We walked around for a bit, but the sun was too hot and the sounds of summer too distracting, so we went inside and sat at the back of the church, where it was cool and dark.

'There's nothing going on with me and Zara,' he said and I scoffed. The evidence had been right there for the whole world to see. How could he deny it? He knew I didn't believe him, but carried on with his defence. 'I admit I kissed her, but there was weird stuff going on at the time. It wasn't a lust thing; it was a comfort thing.'

'And that makes it better, does it?' I didn't know how or why I felt so calm.

'I know it doesn't.' He hung his head. 'But she was just giving me a bit of support.'

'I'm your … *was* your girlfriend …' I said. 'You should have come to me. I've heaped enough junk onto you. Did you really feel you couldn't talk to me about stuff?'

'No,' he said simply. How could such a tiny word hurt so much?

'Why not?' I felt myself deflating. I suddenly didn't feel so strong any more.

''Cos it was about you,' he admitted, though he looked like he didn't want to.

'What do you mean, it was about me?' I stuttered, starting to feel sick 'cos I thought I already knew the answer.

'I needed someone to talk to.' I was stung. He'd talked to *her* about the biggest secret in my world. Was that why she'd started being nice to me again, 'cos she felt sorry for me? I got up to head home. I didn't want to hear any more. I heard him calling for me to go back, but I couldn't.

* * *

I didn't go straight home. I couldn't face it. I needed time to process everything Brian had said and sort it all out in my head. He'd seemed so sincere while we were going out, so why did I suddenly feel that our whole relationship had been a sham? Had he told her everything I'd said? I felt like they'd both been laughing at me all along.

I had been walking for ages when it started to rain. It wasn't just the odd drop here and there; it was like the heavens had opened. I was drenched within seconds. Although I didn't want to, I headed home. My jeans were sticking to my legs and my hair was plastered to my head.

I'd prepared myself to be in trouble when I got home, but when I opened the door, the house was silent and no one was there. I wondered where they'd all got to. I went up to my room to get changed, my head still spinning. Once I'd peeled my clothes off and put my dressing-gown on, I sat heavily on the bed. I didn't want to, but I felt guilty. I couldn't help but feel that I'd lost Brian 'cos I was so weird. I should have known it would be too big for him to understand if I didn't even understand it myself.

The old feelings of hatred and frustration started to seep back in. My whole body filled up with sadness and I felt like it was putting pressure on my heart. It ached and thumped around inside me, and my lungs were struggling to remember how to draw breath.

I started to feel angry with myself. I was a weak person. I was stupid to think that one chat with Rachel would make everything better and make it all go away. This is what always seemed to happen to me. I could be happy and upbeat for a few days, but it would never last. It was almost like I had an in-built ability to mess everything up.

I looked for my box in its usual place and started crying with disappointment in myself when I reached for it. I knew it would make me feel better for a while, but even that didn't last these days, and the feelings of disgust and self-loathing that crept into me through my cuts were almost worse than the feelings of despair I'd had in the first place.

I didn't open it straightaway. I took a deep breath and tried to compose myself. I felt stupid for needing this. They were just a stupid pair of nail scissors. What was the big deal? I tried to reason with myself. If I did it, what would happen? I'd feel all right for ten minutes tops, and then I'd hate myself. I'd hate myself for giving in.

Then I allowed myself to think a thought I'd never had before. What would happen if I didn't do it? Just say I put the box back where it was and left the room? What would happen to me? I had no idea and I didn't know whether I was brave enough to try. Slowly I got up, still gripping onto the box. I wasn't sure if I could do this.

Why should it always end with blood and bandages, and antiseptic? Everyone else seemed to be able to cope without them. It was like there were two Lisas in my head: the self who wanted to cut and the self who wanted to fight the urge. The arguments became jumbled and I was confused.

I couldn't bring myself to let go of the box. Even if I wasn't going to use it, I still needed to hold onto it for security. I decided to go downstairs and wait for my family in the lounge. I'd never do it in such a public place. There was no way I'd risk any of them walking in and finding me.

I knelt on the floor in front of the coffee table and put the box in front of me. I was too scared to take my eyes off it in case the scissors inside jumped out and cut me when I wasn't looking. I was scared I'd like it if that happened, scared it would get hold of me all over again and suck me back in.

I tried to think of the good things in my life. My family loved me, Ellie was home, I'd probably done well in my exams and I had Rachel. Every time a bad thought tried to sneak in, I chased it away with a happy memory. It was working, but I had to concentrate really hard. If I broke the spell, it would get me. I just wished Ellie would get home soon. I wanted her with me. She made it all safe.

'There you are. You were gone for ages. Everyone's out looking for you,' said a dripping Lee as he came in and flicked the lights on. I hadn't noticed it get dark. 'Hope you told Brian where to go. Loser!' he said bitterly, as he took his jacket off and threw it over the back of a chair. When I didn't reply, he turned to look at me properly.

'You okay?' he asked when he noticed me staring. He followed my gaze to the box on the table and although I don't think he knew, he definitely suspected what was inside. 'Lisa?' His voice was a little louder. He was trying to snap me out of it. It was like he was scared to wake a sleepwalker. He came and knelt beside me, and gently put his arm around me, whispering that it was okay; he was there.

Him touching me so softly was like the connection that completed the circuit. Suddenly, the tears came rushing into my eyes, blurring them so much I couldn't see the box any more. I turned to Lee and flung my arms around his neck, sobbing.

'What's he said? What's that jerk done to you?' he asked. I sensed fear in his voice.

'Nothing,' I choked. Lee didn't believe me.

'Just tell me, Lise, and I can help. Have you hurt yourself again?' His face looked tense as he asked. I shook my head and I heard him exhale with relief.

'I nearly did,' I wailed. 'I was going to do it. I'm never going to be able to stop, am I?' The words kept catching in my throat and mixing with the tears.

'Hey,' he said, pulling my arms from around his neck and looking me right in the eye. 'Don't you see what you've done?' He was smiling now and I wondered why. 'You did stop. Look …' He grabbed the box. It was still closed. 'See, it's still closed. You didn't do it. You stopped yourself.' He hugged me, proud of his little sis. I hadn't realized until that moment that he was right. I had fought my demon and won – for the first time.

Epilogue

The idea of stopping for good terrified me, but Lee made me realize that stopping for now was a pretty good start. Looking back, that knowledge was the best birthday present I ever had. Of course, I do still have my down times, and I know self-harm will always be lurking around me, but as long as I know it's there, I can keep it at bay. It can only get me again if I give it permission and I'm not about to do that.

HOLLYOAKS: LUKE'S SECRET DIARY
After 15 March 2000, Luke will ever be the same again. Containing his intimate thoughts as he progresses from cocky wide-boy and star of the football field to rape victim, this is Luke's story in his own words.
ISBN 0 7522 7210 1 £3.99

HOLLYOAKS: THE LIVES AND LOVES OF FINN
Who is Finn: a convict's son? A man who would sleep with his mate's mum? Someone who'd cheat on his girlfriend? Or is he all of these...? This is the inside story of one of *Hollyoaks* most popular characters.
ISBN 0 7522 7211 X £3.99

HOLLYOAKS: STOLEN E-MAILS
When personal e-mails turn up in the wrong inboxes, suspicion grips Hollyoaks. Who is stirring up trouble by redirecting mail? Accusations fly but all the while the mystery hacker is uncovering secrets that could tear people's lives apart...
ISBN 0 7522 1955 3 £4.99

HOLLYOAKS: LUKE'S JOURNAL: A NEW BEGINNING
In this sequel to *Luke's Secret Diary* Luke is trying to pick up the pieces after the rape. But when the trial causes terrible repercussions for the Morgans, and Mandy wants to be just friends, he realises leaving the past behind him isn't that easy...
ISBN 0 7522 1954 5 £4.99

HOLLYOAKS: RUNNING WILD
You're seventeen, strong-willed and sassy. You're on holiday in Ibiza having the time of your life, when suddenly it occurs to you – why go home? In *Running Wild*, Ellie reveals all about her life abroad, while Dan, Gary and Toby reveal what happened to those she left behind.
ISBN 07522 6474 5 £4.99

HOLLYOAKS: THE OFFICIAL COMPANION
Packed with glossy photographs of all your favourite faces, past and present, this is the definitive guide to the hit Channel 4 soap. Take a journey back in time as we linger on classic moments in *Hollyoaks* history, and take in unforgettable characters on the way; read interviews with the cast, articles from the *College Review*, and O.B.'s coursework; find out how *Hollyoaks* is made – and then test yourself with the ultimate *Hollyoaks* quiz! It's all here in this official companion.
ISBN 07522 2000 4 £9.99

**You can order copies direct from the
Channel 4 Shop by calling 0870 1234 344**